The Lost Steps

The Lost Steps
André Breton
Les Pas perdus

Translated by Mark Polizzotti

University of Nebraska Press: Lincoln & London

Publication of this translation
was assisted by a grant from the
French Ministry of Culture.

Acknowledgments for the use of
copyrighted material appear on
pages 127–30.

♾ The paper in this book meets
the minimum requirements of
American National Standard for
Information Sciences – Perma-
nence of Paper for Printed Library Materials, ANSI Z39.48-1984.

Library of Congress
Cataloging in Publication Data
Breton, André, 1896–1966.
[Pas perdus. English] The lost
steps = Les pas perdus / André
Breton ; translated by Mark
Polizzotti. p. cm. – (French mod-
ernist library) Includes index.
ISBN 0-8032-1242-9 (cloth : alk.
paper) I. Polizzotti, Mark. II. Title.
III. Series. PQ2603.R35P313 1997
844'.912–dc20 96-3479 CIP

ISBN 978-0-8032-2814-6
(paper : alk. paper)

CONTENTS

Foreword

This book occupies a special place in our French Modernist Library, which already contains many Surrealist publications, for it is a pivotal work, crucial in the history of both the Dada and the Surrealist movements. It reveals not only Breton's evolution from one to the other and the power of the models he took, some of which he eventually discarded, but also the potential he saw in certain of the paths he tried and the false steps he took along others. It is an exploration of steps lost and found—Breton's equivalent, in some ways, of Proust's own search for his lost time. Breton, in finding his path after the long pacing up and down, found and founded the Surrealist movement, without which our century would have been different indeed. These essays form the path of the finding of that path.

In these pages Breton shows a kind of humor—related to Jacque Vaché's *umor*—that will be less in evidence later. Its aesthetic impact can be judged from a letter Vaché wrote to Breton on 18 August 1917: "And then the TONE of our gesture remains to be decided—I would like it dry, without any literature, and above all not in the sense of ART."[1] Compared to Vaché, many of the figures in the creative world around Breton seem dull and bourgeois to him, as they commit the daily and unforgivable crime of

1. Jacques Vaché, *Lettres de guerre* (Paris: Eric Losfeld, 1970), 57. See the authoritative discussions in the Pléïade edition of Breton's works (*Oeuvres complètes,* ed. Marguerite Bonnet, with Philippe Bernier, Marie-Claire Dumas, Etienne-Alain Hubert, and José Pierre [Paris: Gallimard, "Bibliothèque de la Pléïade," 1988]) and Bonnet's crucially important *André Breton: Naissance de l'aventure surréaliste* (Paris: José Corti, 1975; English translation by Paul Lenti published as part of *4 Dada Suicides* [London: Atlas, 1995]).

mediocrity: they have "settled down," as he intends never to do. Breton's other heroes, like Alfred Jarry, the creator of *Ubu Rex,* are as antisocial as Vaché, but their protests leave a literary trace, as Vaché's have the merit of not doing.

In this Dada/Surrealist universe it is the path that finds the steps to trace it. Consequently Breton's sometimes arrogant exaltations are possible precisely and only within this uncharted exploration of divergent routes. Later, of course, these paths had to find their place on a map and their relation to each other. In the moment of this publication, however, there is a kind of freedom in the disparate judgments with their occasional naïveté, their frequent lashing out, and their peculiar unfairness (see "Interview with Doctor Freud"!) that delight the quirky soul. I first loved Breton through these steps, which never seemed false to me and whose errancies I cherished, in the same way I cherished, say, the wandering steps of Gongora, to which that other great Surrealist, Robert Desnos, refers in his own path-making writings.

In any case, this Breton is not yet to be accused of popery and overcertainty; this is a Breton you can care about, argue with, and be amused by. This is not yet a Breton ruling over his *mandarin curaçao* and his group in their various cafés. The chosen way leading from one prescribed café to another, the certainty about what is and is not Surrealist—none of that is here yet: the steps are not yet marked.

I do not mean to imply that Breton's wit or spontaneity died out later; rather, he occasionally forgot—perhaps disdained—to give them such free rein. There were too many serious things going on then. This is a young man's wit, just at the beginning of things, a young man's self-assurance, and his doubt, too. The quite extraordinary way that Breton dwells on his early hero Jacques Vaché bears its own witness to that doubt. Breton's willing and lifelong projection of himself onto something or someone else is a great part of his attraction for us. His enthusiasm, which sometimes had to carry an entire group, is the mark of a generous spirit, the other side of which is that intellectual and emotional certainty stated in the tone of the extreme: "Pardon me for thinking that, unlike ivy, I die when I become attached."

This testament that Breton left of his mental evolution from the Dada movement to the formulation of the Surrealist movement bears witness to an epoch, a state of mind, and an intellectual spirit turned toward the new. Describing their general content, Breton calls these writings "a collection of essays on the tendencies and personalities of our epoch: dadaism, surrealism, 'the new spirit,' seen above all from the moral point of view." And indeed, they are concerned more with questions of how and why to live than with any conception of how to write or of any settled literary and artistic activity.

It is against any settling at all that the essays in *The Lost Steps* are assembled, the idea of wandering and meandering already expressing the state of expectation that characterizes Surrealism at its best. This work is the perfect prefiguration of the waiting state, even as it is the perfect figuration of a transition. The essay most nearly approximating Breton's open state of mind announces a general departure: "Leave Everything"—a phrase appropriate for train stations like the Gare de Lyon, where, to use the memorable image that Breton will later offer, the train is always shaking with convulsive beauty, always just about to leave.

What Breton claims to be leaving here is not only Dada, with its ardor for the unexpected and its taste for negation. He is also leaving that kind of negative collective temperament that Dada was, as defined mostly by Tzara, not just to commit himself to a waiting room or to marking time but to find his own individual poetic sensibility. He leaves Dada for another state of mind, one not yet defined as Surrealism but significant by virtue of being something else. What he finds will be summed up in the optimistic words *mad love* and the optimistic image of communicating vessels, in the belief in the power of language to remake the universe,[2] and in the paradoxical, impossible, and no less optimistic expression "Always for the first time."

Nothing is to tarnish or have its surprise wear off: this is the point of the "new spirit," in homage to which the last essay in this collection was written. This address to an audience in Barcelona in 1922 is a monument of self-concern, self-confession, and self-importance. As a preface to the Surrealist movement about to be born, it is the supreme document of a moment as well as a spirit, questioning the nature and value of art, life, and the human mind. It is good that Surrealism, one of whose greatest temptations was to be that of too much certainty, should have begun with these meandering steps and these questions: nothing of them will be lost.

MARY ANN CAWS

2. "Doesn't the mediocrity of our universe depend essentially on our powers of evocation?" Breton will ask in 1925. He was never to lose his faith in language.

Preface:
Steps Meandering and Guided

"Lost steps? But there's no such thing!" Breton's heroine Nadja exclaims in response to the book he hands her. She is right, of course, but only if we stick with her literal reading. Actually, the title—*Les Pas perdus* in the original—evokes not so much loss (although this, too, is present) as aimlessness; it inevitably recalls for its French audience the locution *salle des pas perdus,* the waiting room of a train station, where expectant travelers errantly pace. Like many of Breton's titles, this one acts as a billboard: the following writings, individually and as a whole, form above all a record of imminent departure.

Originally published in February 1924, *The Lost Steps* is the first of Breton's four essay collections. Like its sequels, it gathers the best of his short prose from the preceding years and sums up a defined period in the author's life. The present pieces were composed between 1917 and 1923, when Breton was between the ages of twenty-one and twenty-seven. They chronicle the path leading from his earliest adult enthusiasms, through his passage into and out of the tumultuous Dada movement, and finally to the mixture of personal anecdote and programmatic assertion that directly foreshadows, and directly precedes, the *Manifesto of Surrealism*.

Because these essays are arranged essentially in chronological order (with one notable exception), it is possible for us to retrace that path—all the more so if we see them as falling into four more or less discrete groups: the early, consciously erudite critiques of a writer's life and work; the defense and illustration of Dada and of its spokesman, Tristan Tzara; the subsequent ejection and denigration of Dada, along with much of Breton's past; and the

exploration and definition of what would soon become the Surrealist movement.

The earliest essays—particularly the extended commentaries on
Apollinaire and Jarry—were written while Breton was a medical
intern during World War I. They are an odd group in the context
of *The Lost Steps:* in terms of style, none can boast the self-assurance and brashness that mark the best of Breton's writings from
this period. At the same time, they demonstrate, with a clarity
that few of the other pieces manage, his broad knowledge and
deep understanding of the authors he most admired. There is a
true deference in these texts, a desire to keep the subject front
and center, while Breton himself uncharacteristically retreats behind the curtain of his presentation. What makes this deference
rather curious in Apollinaire's case is that Breton's admiration
was already subtended by not inconsiderable doubts.

Breton had first met Apollinaire in May 1916, as the latter was
recovering from a serious head wound. Their relations, although
they continued regularly until Apollinaire's death in November
1918 (less than a month after "Guillaume Apollinaire" was first
published), were nonetheless pocked with a fair share of am-
bivalence on Breton's part: he loved the poet's innovative spirit
but was dismayed by the man's conformist attitudes toward the
war and official honors. Still, there are few traces of these mis-
givings in Breton's presentation. On the contrary, he seems delib-
erately to avoid saying anything that might offend the mentor
—so much so that Breton's friend Philippe Soupault, another
habitué of Apollinaire's, remembered feeling "a certain embar-
rassment" when he read the article. This resolutely positive spin
stems partly from genuine admiration, partly from the fact that
the text had been commissioned by Apollinaire himself ("I don't
know of anyone who can speak of what I've done as well as you
can," he had told his young friend in March 1917), and partly, no
doubt, from youthful opportunism. As a virtually unpublished
writer of twenty-one, Breton was clearly flattered by Apollinaire's
offer, and still more so by his ambitious plans for the text: it

was to run in the prestigious *Mercure de France* and to serve as an introduction to a planned anthology of the poet's writings (although neither ultimately happened). Only after Apollinaire's death did Breton start tempering his affection in print—to the point, in "Characteristics of the Modern Evolution" (1922), of singling out his former mentor for special repudiation.

Apollinaire was not the first literary figure to win Breton's esteem. In the two years before their first meeting, Breton had invested a similar interest in Paul Valéry (a relation that inspired several youthful poems in the manner of the Symbolists, but no critical articles). During roughly the same period he also became a protégé of the Cubist poet Pierre Reverdy, who edited the literary magazine *Nord-Sud* and published some of his early verse. Less directly, but no less ardently, Breton developed a passion for the lives and works of both Alfred Jarry and Isidore Ducasse, the self-styled "Comte de Lautréamont," with, at least in Jarry's case, as much emphasis on the human anecdote as on the literary product. By far the most decisive encounter of those years, however, was with a fellow soldier named Jacques Vaché.

Barely six months older than Breton, Vaché already bore the air of someone who had seen it all and could no longer care about any of it. As Breton recounted some thirty-five years later, they met "in a hospital in Nantes, where I was an intern and he was being treated. This was in the early months of 1916. I was struck both by the very studied character of his countenance and by the ultracasual tone of his statements. . . . In Vaché's person, in utmost secrecy, a principle of total insubordination was undermining the world, reducing everything that seemed all-important to a petty scale."

One of Vaché's main weapons in his private war against conformity was the notion he dubbed *umor,* a forerunner of what Breton later termed *black humor.* "I believe it is a sensation—I almost said a SENSE—that too—of the theatrical (and joyless) pointlessness of everything," Vaché explained in April 1917, in what has now become a celebrated formula. This particular brand of *umor* found its expression less in Vaché's scant written output—which for all intents and purposes constitutes a slim volume of "letters from the front" (mostly to Breton) and two brief stories—than in his living actions and attitudes, as Breton faithfully preserved them on paper and in conversation. "We were those joyful terrorists, hardly more sentimental than was fashionable," he says in the first of several portraits of his friend.

Vaché's example informs a number of these texts, and not only the ones specifically devoted to him. "All the literary or artistic cases that I'm forced to consider take their place behind him," Breton writes in "The Disdainful Confession," "and even then they hold my attention only insofar as I can measure their human significance against this infinite scale." The young man's death in January 1919—a death that Breton considered to have been willful suicide, although much of the evidence suggests otherwise—was one of the defining traumas of Breton's life. With Vaché ended the kind of strictly literary attachment that had inspired such scholarly studies as "Guillaume Apollinaire" and "Alfred Jarry," paving the way for the complete revision of values that would come with Dada's installation in Paris the following spring. "If not for [Vaché], I might have become a poet," Breton notes in memoriam. "He overcame in me the conspiracy of dark forces that makes one believe he can have anything as absurd as a vocation."

Coming less than a year after his first recollection of Vaché, the essay entitled "Two Dada Manifestoes" is Breton's earnest if slightly awkward attempt to match his native sobriety ("the naturally recalcitrant spirit I bring to things") with Tristan Tzara's manic, scattershot energy. Breton had begun corresponding with Tzara in early 1919, immediately after receiving news of Vaché's death, a coincidence that was not lost on him. "If I have an insane confidence in you, it's because you remind me of a friend, my best friend, Jacques Vaché, who died several months ago," he wrote in one of his first letters to the Dadaist leader. Decades afterward, in *Conversations,* Breton admitted to interviewer André Parinaud that it was this perceived resemblance, rather than any clear view of Tzara himself, that led him "to transfer onto [Tzara] much of the confidence and hope that I had placed in Vaché."

At the beginning of 1920, when Tzara transplanted Dada from Zurich to Paris, Breton eagerly handed over to him his activities, his friends, and *Littérature,* the magazine that he had recently co-founded with Philippe Soupault and Louis Aragon. For the next six months he seconded Tzara in his assaults on French cultural complacency, notably by participating in a variety of Dada "demonstrations" whose standard features included incoherent plays and sketches, disjointed music, shouting matches with the audience, and, always, a copious number of recited manifestoes. The two manifestoes reprinted here were originally published as part of a special issue of *Littérature* devoted to Dada's public pronouncements. And already, despite the enthusiasm, they show signs of the irreconcilable divergences between Breton's viewpoint and Dada's that would erupt two years later. His entries reflect a logical discursiveness that differs sharply from, say, Tzara's exhortation: "Look at me! I'm an idiot, I'm a trickster, I'm a practical joker. Look at me! I'm ugly, my face wears no expression, I'm short. I'm like all the rest of you!"

Three months later, in August, Breton took a more genuine, if still less Dadaist, approach to the movement in "For Dada," published this time in the established literary monthly *La Nouvelle Revue Française.* Although the piece may employ the same staccato style as the two manifestoes, it does away with much of the gratuitous provocativeness in favor of a more grounded reflection. Statements such as "Almost every true imagistic innovation . . . strikes me as being a spontaneous creation," or Breton's discussion of the critics' misperceptions of Dada, place the debate on a much less frenetic plane, opening Dada to precisely the kind of rational exegesis that could only corrode it from within.

In fact, by the time he wrote this article, Breton was having serious doubts about Dada's viability. As he recalled for André Parinaud, he "came away [from the demonstrations] rather discontented, hardly proud of the pitiful carnival ruses we'd needed in order to attract the public. . . . The Dada magazines and performances stagnated under Tzara's leadership . . . they became stereotyped, ossified." His allegiance to the movement and to Tzara would persist for another year or so, ever flagging, until events in early 1922 ended it completely.

Breton's final break with Dada, reflected in the editorials "After Dada," "Leave Everything," and "Clearly," occurred over his attempts in January 1922 to found a "congress for the determination and defense of the modern spirit" (also known as the Congress of Paris). Bored with Tzara's taste for repetitive gags and endless publicity, and resentful of his leadership, Breton decided to organize a mammoth conference involving as many prominent European intellectuals as he could attract. His ambition was to clarify, through a series of lectures and roundtables, the major tendencies of modern artistic expression—and less explicitly, to deflect the avant-garde's attention away from Tzara and onto himself. But the project collapsed even before it began, owing (in Breton's view) to the "endless" preparations, the "astonishing vanity of each of its members," and especially, to sabotage by Tzara, "who did not find any personal benefit in all this and whose head, as usual, had been turned by a few press clippings." In reality it was Breton himself who most undermined his congress: after offering Tzara a place on the steering committee, which Tzara publicly declined, he attacked his former comrade as "a publicity-mongering imposter . . . known as the promoter of a 'movement' that comes from Zurich." To the congress's international constituency such remarks smacked a little too much of xenophobia, and Breton's enterprise succumbed to a general withdrawal of support. Breton remained bitter over the failure, and his editorials of the next several months contain a perceptibly heightened quotient of spleen.

Coinciding with the break from Dada, the snide interviews with Gide and Freud equally betray the sting of defeated expectation. Breton, as he says of himself, had "never been a familiar of André Gide's," but he had greatly admired his character Lafcadio (from the 1914 novel *Lafcadio's Adventures*), whose youthful nihilism seemed to foretoken the unsparing nonchalance of Jacques Vaché. By the time the interview was published, however, Breton had become disenchanted with Gide's arrogation of posterity and miffed by the novelist's own snubbing of the Congress of Paris. His response was to reproduce fragments of their conversation, apparently verbatim, arranged in such a way as to make Gide look like a vainglorious buffoon, a response that left Gide feeling wounded and confused and that put a stop to their relations for a number of years.

Matters went a little deeper with Freud, for in this case Breton sincerely hoped to win the analyst's approval for what he saw as his own contributions to the theory of the unconscious. In 1920 he had sent Freud a dedicated copy of his and Soupault's book *The Magnetic Fields*, composed entirely of automatic writings. With such raw materials, Breton felt, psychoanalysis could take its studies of literary texts much further than it had previously done, and he expected Freud to agree. Freud, however, did not really see the interest of such blatantly manifest content, nor could he fathom what this obscure French poet wanted from him. Breton nonetheless arranged to visit the eminent Austrian, taking advantage of his honeymoon trip to Vienna in October 1921 and still expecting to be greeted as a fellow explorer of the hidden mind. In nervous anticipation he paced around Freud's house for several days "without finding the resolve to knock," as he reported to a friend. "I'm carrying such a reassuring photograph of him." When it finally took place, however, the actual meeting so disappointed Breton that afterward he refused to talk about it, not even to his bride, who had been waiting for him in a café down the street. The only written trace of the event is the terse "Interview with Doctor Freud," published the following year, in which his interlocutor is described as "a little old man with no style who receives clients in a shabby office worthy of the neighborhood GP." Although Breton would try several more times to interest Freud in Surrealism, sending him copies of his books and seeking to recruit him for various projects, Freud would never move beyond his stance of kindly skepticism, nor Breton beyond his of offended spite.

This clean sweep of the past marks a primary transition point in *The Lost Steps*, the point at which Breton stopped looking rearward and began qualifying exactly what the future might hold for him and his friends. Articles such as "Reply to a Survey" and "Distance" directly address current literary and artistic affairs, offering a first glimpse of what the Surrealist view of these issues would be (significantly, both were published in daily newspapers rather than in the more specialized magazines that typically welcomed Breton's editorials). And in the discussions of Duchamp and Picabia, we can see crucial differences between Breton's approach in late 1922 and that of his wartime articles on Apollinaire and Jarry: whereas the earlier pieces seek mainly to give a comprehensive overview, these later ones present their subjects as the embodiment and proof of a burgeoning zeitgeist.

Nor is it accidental that both Picabia and Duchamp can be seen as the great precursors-cum-survivors of Dada, the former through his mercurial ties to the movement (and at least at the time of the essay's composition, through his alliance with Breton against their former friend Tzara) and the latter through his casual skirting of any formal allegiance whatsoever. To argue that these two "harbingers" had discovered many of Dada's tenets several years before Tzara's 1918 manifesto—a claim Breton also makes for Jacques Vaché—not only damps much of Dada's original fire; it also throws open once more the entire plane of investigation. Dada, in this light, becomes just another failed attempt to capitalize on the "modern spirit." What Breton offers in its stead is something else entirely.

This something else takes two main forms in *The Lost Steps*, both of which would become touchstones of Surrealism in its early phase. The first involves experiments with what the *Manifesto* calls "psychic automatism." As noted earlier, Breton had already explored the dark byways of automatic writing, emerging with the texts that constituted *The Magnetic Fields*. In the intervening years, however, he had become disillusioned with the results he and his friends were obtaining:

Nevermore after [The Magnetic Fields], *on the occasions when we awaited this murmur in hopes of capturing it for precise ends, did it take us very far. And yet such had been its power that I expect nothing else to afford a greater revelation. . . . I had recently decided that the incursions of conscious elements in this domain, which would place it under a well-determined human or literary will, would subject it to the sort of exploitation that could bear only less and less fruit. I would soon lose all interest in it.*

In search of new avenues, Breton at this point began holding spiritualist "séances." The impetus came from his once and future collaborator René Crevel, who had himself been initiated only weeks before. Although Breton professed little interest in the aims of spiritualism—"I absolutely refuse to admit that any communication whatsoever can exist between the living and the dead," he declares in "The Mediums Enter"—he immediately saw the induced slumbers as a remarkable illustration of the mind's creative resources. For the next several months (until the violent behavior of some participants caused him to suspend the activity once and for all), these slumbers seemed to Breton an ideal solution to the problem of soliciting the unconscious oracle, and the séances were held on an almost nightly basis, with ever more thrilling results. "A dazzling new day is dawning," he announced in a letter of the time.

With similar optimism Breton presents the poet Robert Desnos's spooneristic word games in "Words without Wrinkles." Desnos, who shortly before had distinguished himself in the arena of induced slumbers (so much so that he and Crevel soon fell into a bitter rivalry), now tried to go one better by spinning sentence after sentence of complicated puns, which he claimed were telepathically communicated to him from New York by Marcel Duchamp. Desnos even appropriated Duchamp's alter ego, Rrose Sélavy, as the heroine of his utterances. Breton seems to have put little stock in Desnos's claims of telepathy, but he was profoundly moved by such products as "Could the solution of a sage be the pollution of a page?" and "The acts of sexes are the axis of sects," to give perhaps the only two that survive translation relatively intact. Although he later judged these phrases to be "marred by facilities, even trivialities," he never disavowed "their completely inspired, irrepressible, inexhaustible nature."

Taken together, these twin explorations of the unconscious, particularly in the context of the automatic writings and dream narratives that had preceded them, form the matrix of what was already being labeled "Surrealism." But *The Lost Steps* contains one final indicator of the road to come, significantly placed at the head of the volume. Written in the spring of 1923 (therefore last), "The Disdainful Confession" both encompasses "the tendencies and figures of our age" (as Breton described it to one newspaper) and, stylistically, prefigures the semidiscursive, semi-anecdotal approach that characterizes such major works as *Nadja* (1928), *The Communicating Vessels* (1932), and *Mad Love* (1937). Breton begins by passing in review a number of his attitudes toward such matters as ethical philosophy, intelligence and logic, the allure of hazard ("Every night I would leave the door to my hotel room wide open in hopes of finally waking beside a companion I hadn't chosen"), and the compromises that both society and human nature try to wring out of an individual. The culmination of these various attitudes (as Nadja would be several years later, and after her Jacqueline Lamba in *Mad Love*) is Breton's meeting and brief friendship with Jacques Vaché, who here, as Breton later said of him, "cut[s] the figure of an enlightener." Lucid, unsentimental, and heartfelt, the valedictory portrait of Vaché that ends the piece yields some of the most affecting pages Breton ever wrote. However "disdainful" his confession might be, in its hopes and its tragedies, its bravery and fears, it casts a strange and brilliant light over the two dozen subsequent essays, providing a context in which they can be properly understood and giving the collection as a whole its guiding thread.

It is this thread, gossamer and hemp by turns, that Breton follows here, like some Theseus in a labyrinth built by centuries of artistic stagnation, tended by the Minotaur of cultural prejudice. That he occasionally takes a false step is as undeniable as it is unavoidable. But for the most part, his footfalls, at once wandering and directed, echo throughout this book with the promising noise of revolutions forever unfinished and departures forever renewed.[1]

MARK POLIZZOTTI

1. In preparing this translation I was aided by the work of two scholars in particular. The first is the late Marguerite Bonnet, editor of the Pléiade edition of Breton's complete works, who amassed a vast array of documents relating to the genesis and writing of *The Lost Steps.* I have made occasional use of her annotations, both in negotiating some of the more obscure detours of Breton's prose and in preparing the notes to this volume. The second is Mary Ann Caws, whose previous, unpublished translation of these essays gave welcome reassurance and who provided some notes of her own. I gratefully acknowledge my debt to both.

Unless otherwise indicated, notes in the text are Breton's. Titles of literary works cited by him are given in English when such a translation exists or, failing this, in the original.

Finally, a word about the title: given my remarks in the opening paragraph of this introduction, one might reasonably argue that I should have called the American edition something like "errant steps" or "wanderings." If I have finally ceded to my preference for the more literal *Lost Steps,* it is both because the work is already referred to as such in several English-language writings and because the present title incorporates (as does Breton's original) a note of wistfulness lacking in the more footloose alternatives.

The Lost Steps

The Disdainful Confession

Sometimes, to signify "experience," we might say that a person has a solid head on his shoulders. You can see how such a solidity might entail the displacement of the person's center of gravity. We are even used to thinking of this solidity as the very condition of human equilibrium—a completely relative equilibrium, since, at least theoretically, the functional assimilation that characterizes living beings ends when the favorable conditions cease, as they always do. I am twenty-seven years old, and I flatter myself with not having known this equilibrium for very long. I have always forbidden myself to think of the future; and if I've considered taking on a project now and again, it was purely as a favor to certain individuals, and only I knew what deep reservations I harbored. Still, I do not mean to suggest that I'm indifferent to these projects, nor do I find anything reassuring in the belief that all is vanity. Absolutely incapable of settling for the fate allotted to me, struck in my highest degree of awareness by the denial of justice that the notion of original sin, to my mind, in no way excuses, I refuse to adapt my existence to the pitiful conditions under which everyone *here below* must exist. On that score, I completely agree with men such as Benjamin Constant before his return from Italy, or with Tolstoy when he said, "If a man has learned to think, it hardly matters what he is thinking; at bottom he is always thinking about his own death. All the philosophers were like that. And what truth can there be, if there is death?"

I will not sacrifice anything to happiness: pragmatism is not within my power. To seek comfort in a given belief strikes me as vulgar. It is beneath contempt to suppose that there is a remedy to moral suffering. I consider suicide legitimate in only one case:

having no challenge to make the world other than *desire,* having no greater challenge laid out to me than death, I can reach the point of desiring death. But the issue is not to sink into stupidity, for that would mean giving myself over to remorse. I tried that once or twice: it doesn't suit me.

Desire . . . the man who said, "Breton: sure of never having finished with his heart, the knob on his door," was certainly not mistaken. I have been criticized for my enthusiasm, and it's true that I pass easily from the keenest interest to sheer indifference—which is not always appreciated by those around me. In literature I have fallen in love by turns with Rimbaud, Jarry, Apollinaire, Nouveau, and Lautréamont, but it is to Jacques Vaché that I am most indebted. The hours I spent with him in Nantes in 1916 seem almost magical. I will never lose sight of him, and although I'm still capable of forming attachments to the various people I meet, I know I will never belong to anyone else with such abandon. If not for him, I might have become a poet. He overcame in me the conspiracy of dark forces that makes one believe he can have anything as absurd as a vocation. I am pleased, in turn, to have something to do with the fact that several young writers today have lost all literary ambition. We *publish* to seek out men, nothing more. With each day I am more and more curious to find these men.

My curiosity, moreover, which can focus passionately on certain individuals, is rather difficult to arouse. I have no great respect for erudition or even—no matter what ridicule this admission will call down on me—for culture. I received an average education, which was almost useless. At most I have retained a fairly sure sense of certain things (some have gone so far as to claim that I have a special gift for the French language, an opinion that never fails to annoy me). In short I know enough to serve my own particular needs vis-à-vis human knowledge.

I tend to think, along with Barrès, that "the great concern, for the preceding generations, was the passage from the absolute to the relative" and that "today, the issue is to move from doubt to

negation without at the same time losing all sense of ethical value."
The question of ethics preoccupies me. The naturally recalcitrant
spirit I bring to things would incline me to subordinate this question to the psychological result, if I didn't sometimes think it to
be superior to the debate. Its advantage, for me, is that it keeps
reason in check, even as it allows for the widest mental deviations.
I love all the ethical philosophers, particularly Vauvenargues and
Sade. Ethics is the great conciliator. To attack it is still to pay it
homage. In it I have always found my main sources of elation.

On the other hand, I do not see so-called logic as anything
more than the shameful exercise of weakness. Without affecta-
tion, I can say that consistency in my opinions is the least of my
worries. Einstein tells us that "one event cannot be the cause of
another unless you can bring them both about in the same point
of space." That is roughly what I have always believed. As long as
I am touching the ground, I can deny things; at a certain altitude
I can be in love; what would I do higher up? And still, in any
one of those states, I have never passed through the same point
twice; when I write "touching the ground," "at a certain altitude,"
"higher up," I am not taken in by my images.

This said, I make no claim to intelligence. I argue more or less in-
stinctively from within a given reasoning, or some other vicious
circle. (Pierre is not necessarily mortal. Beneath the apparent de-
duction that allows us to establish the contrary lies a rather paltry
trick. It is quite obvious that the first proposition—all men are
mortal—is a sophism.) But nothing is further from me than the
care certain individuals take to preserve what can be preserved.
In this regard youth is a marvelous talisman. I take the liberty of
referring my opponents in the debate (if I have any) to the dire
warning in the opening pages of *Adolphe:* "I found that no goal
was worth the required effort. It is rather curious that this impression has weakened precisely as my years have increased. Could it
be that there is something dubious about hope, and that when it
withdraws from a man's life, this life takes on a sterner but more
positive character?"

I have sworn, in any case, not to let anything become dulled in me as long as I have a choice.

All the same, I notice how skillfully nature tries to get me to make all sorts of concessions. Behind the mask of boredom, doubt, or necessity, it tries to extort some act of renunciation, in exchange for which it offers me no end of inducements. It used to be that I never left home without saying farewell to all the binding memories that had accumulated there, to everything that I felt ready to perpetuate in myself. The street, which I believed could furnish my life with its surprising detours; the street, with its cares and its glances, was my true element: there I could test like nowhere else the winds of possibility.

Every night I would leave the door to my hotel room wide open in hopes of finally waking beside a companion I hadn't chosen. Only later did I fear that that street and that unknown woman would in turn tie me down, but that is another matter. To tell the truth, I am not sure you can win this never-ending struggle, its usual outcome being the stagnation of everything that is most spontaneous and precious in the world. Apollinaire, whose clear-sightedness rarely failed him, was ready to make any sacrifice in the months preceding his death; Valéry, who earlier had nobly announced his will to silence, is now letting himself go with utter abandon, authorizing the worst forgeries of his thought, not to mention his work. Hardly a week goes by that some admirable mind does not "fall into line." It seems that one can behave with greater or lesser degrees of honor, and that's all. I do not yet care to know which cart I'm to be taken away in or how long I can hold out. Until further notice, anything that can delay the categorization of beings or ideas—that can, in a word, maintain ambiguity—has my full approval. My greatest desire is to apply to myself, for as long as possible, Lautréamont's admirable phrase: "Since the unmentionable day of my birth, I have pledged an irreconcilable hatred against the somniferous bedboards."

"Why do you write?" is the question that *Littérature* once decided to ask some so-called literary lights. Soon afterward the magazine extracted the most satisfactory answer from Lieutenant Glahn's notebook, in *Pan:* "I write," said Glahn, "because it shortens the time." This is the only answer to which I can still subscribe, with the caveat that I also believe I write because it lengthens time. In any case, I claim to act on it, and I offer as proof the continuation I once gave to this development of a thought by Pascal: "Those who judge a work by some rule are, compared to the others, like those who have a watch compared to those who do not." I went on: "One of them, consulting his watch, says, 'We have been here for two hours.' The other one, consulting his watch, says, 'It's been only forty-five minutes.' I have no watch. I say to the first, 'You're bored,' and to the second, 'Time passes quickly for you,' because I think it has been an hour and a half. And I laugh at those who say that time passes slowly for me and that I am judging by my watch: they don't know that I am judging by pure whim."

I, who let no line flow from my pen in which I do not see some distant meaning, ascribe no importance *whatsoever* to posterity. Moreover, public figures after their death are no doubt prey to increasing indifference. Some people these days already do not know whom to rely on. No one grooms his legend anymore. . . . Quite a few lives refuse to reach any moral conclusion. When the thought of Rimbaud or Ducasse stops being considered a problem (to who knows what childish ends), when the "teachings" of the war of 1914 have been sufficiently absorbed, we can presumably allow ourselves to concede that writing history is pointless. More and more we are realizing that re-creation is impossible. On top of which, it is clear that no one truth deserves to remain exemplary. I am not among those who say "In my day"; I simply affirm that *any* thinking person can only lead his fellows astray. And I am not seeking for myself a fate better than the one I would allot to anyone else.

This is how we should understand the *dictatorship of the mind,* which was one of Dada's catchphrases. From this you can imagine how art interests me only to a relative degree. But today a prejudice that tends to grant to the criterion "human" everything that is being denied the "beautiful" is gaining credibility. And yet there are no degrees of humanity, or else the works of Germain Nouveau would be inferior to those of a Montmartre street singer, and no wonder: Down with the melodrama in which Margot. . . . The only thing I would consider worth doing is escaping, as much as possible, from that human type we all share in. For me, to get away from the psychological rule, to no matter how small a degree, is equivalent to inventing new ways of feeling. Even with all the disappointments it has already caused me, I still see poetry as the terrain on which the terrible difficulties that consciousness has with confidence, in a given individual, have the best chance of being resolved. That is why I occasionally act so harshly toward it, why I can forgive it no abdication. The role it has to play stands beyond philosophy, and it betrays its mission each time it falls under the sway of a philosophical decree. It is commonly believed that the *meaning* of what my friends and I write has stopped mattering to us, whereas on the contrary we feel that the moral dissertations of someone like Racine are utterly unworthy of the admirable style in which they are couched. Perhaps we are trying to make the *substance* live up to the form again, and so naturally our first impulse is to go beyond practical utility. In the realm of poetry we have scarce more than circumstantial verse under our belts. And besides, isn't the true meaning of a work not the one people think they have given it but rather the one it is liable to take on in relation to its surroundings?

To those who, on the strength of currently fashionable theories, would try to determine what emotional trauma might have turned me into a person who could say such things, I can do no less, before concluding, than dedicate the following portrait, which they can insert into the slim volume of *Letters from the Front* by Jacques Vaché, published in 1918 by Au Sans Pareil.[1] I'm sure that the few facts this portrait helps to reconstruct will illustrate quite nicely the little I have said. It is still very hard to define just what Jacques Vaché meant by "umor" (no *h*) and to clarify

1. The book was actually published in August 1919 and serialized in the July through September issues of Breton's magazine *Littérature*. (trans.)

where we stand with regard to the battle he waged between his capacity for emotion and certain impassive aspects of his character. There will be time later for confronting umor with the kind of poetry that, ultimately, can do without poems: that is, poetry in the sense we understand it. For the moment I will limit myself to relating a few vivid memories.

It was in Nantes, where, in early 1916, I was stationed as a temporary intern at the neurological center, that I first met Jacques Vaché. At the time he was being treated at the hospital on Rue du Boccage for a leg wound. One year older than I, he was a very elegant young man with red hair who had studied with Luc-Olivier Merson at the Ecole des Beaux-Arts. Confined to his bed, he passed the time by drawing and painting a series of postcards, for which he thought up outlandish captions. Men's fashions occupied the bulk of his imagination. He loved the clean-shaven faces and hieratic attitudes you see in bars. Every morning he spent a good hour laying out one or two photographs, a few goblets, and some violets on a small, lace-covered table, just within reach. Back then I was composing poems in the style of Mallarmé. I was going through one of the most difficult periods of my life, beginning to see that I would not be able to do what I wanted. The war dragged on. Auxiliary hospital no. 103-*bis* echoed with the shouts of the doctor on call—a charming fellow, moreover: "Dyspepsia? never heard of it. There are two kinds of stomach ailments: one is certainly cancer; the other, though doubtful, is ulcers. Give him two helpings of meat and salad and he'll get over it. I'll be your death, friend," and so on. Jacques Vaché smiled. We spoke of Rimbaud (whom he had always hated), Apollinaire (with whom he was barely familiar), Jarry (whom he admired), Cubism (which he distrusted). He was stingy with information about his past. I believe that he reproached in me my will toward art and modernism, which since that time . . . but let's not get ahead of ourselves. His attitude bore no trace of snobbery. "Dada" did not exist yet, and Jacques Vaché would never know about it. Consequently, it was he who first insisted on the importance of gestures, which are so dear to Mr. André Gide. The condition of being a soldier is particularly suited to personal effusiveness. Someone who has never been forced to snap to attention cannot know how badly you can long to take to your heels. Jacques Vaché was a past master in the art of "attaching very little importance to anything." He understood that sentimentality was no longer the order of the day and that a proper regard for one's dignity, whose fundamental value hadn't yet been underscored by Charlie Chaplin, required a certain impassiveness. "We needed our air dry, a little," he writes in his letters. In 1916 one barely had time to recognize a friend. Even *behind the lines* meant nothing. All that mattered was to keep living, and the simple fact of polishing rings in the trenches[2] or turning one's head struck us as corrupt. Writing and thinking were no longer enough; above all, one had to cultivate the illusion of movement, of noise.

Scarcely out of the hospital, Jacques Vaché got himself hired as a stevedore and unloaded coal from the Loire. He spent his afternoons in the slums near the port. In the evening he went from café to café, movie house to movie house, dropping inordinate sums of money, creating around himself an atmosphere at once dramatic and vivid, spun from the lies he liked to tell (he introduced me to everyone as André Salmon, because of the minor reputation this writer enjoyed—which I didn't fully appreciate until later). I have to admit that he did not share my enthusiasms and that for a long time he saw me as the "po-wet," someone who hadn't fully absorbed the lesson of the times. He *occasionally* strolled around Nantes in the uniform of a lieutenant in the hussards, or of an airman, or a doctor. It might be that, meeting you on the street, he would pretend not to recognize you and would continue on his way without a backward glance. Vaché never shook hands, to say either hello or goodbye. He lived in Place du Beffroi, in a pretty room with a young woman whom I knew only as Louise and whom, when I visited, he obliged to stand still and silent for hours in a corner. At five o'clock she served

2. An allusion to Apollinaire's poem "The Seasons" (in *Calligrammes*), in which he recounts "polishing till evening incredible rings" in the trenches. (trans.)

tea, and his only thanks was to kiss her hand. As he told it, they had no sexual relations; rather, he was content simply to sleep beside her in the same bed. This was, he assured me, his standard procedure. Still, he seemed to like calling her "my mistress," no doubt anticipating the question that Gide would later ask: "Was Jacques Vaché a virgin?"

Starting in May 1916 I was to see my friend only five or six more times. He had been sent back to the front, from where he would write me sporadically (he who wrote to no one, except, out of self-interest, to his mother every two or three months). On 23 June 1917, returning at around two in the morning to La Pitié hospital, where I was being treated, I found a note from him, along with the drawing that figures as the frontispiece of his *Letters*. He set a date for the following afternoon at the premiere of *Les Mamelles de Tirésias*.

It was at the Conservatoire Maubel that I next saw Jacques Vaché. The first act had just ended. A British officer was making a scene in the orchestra seats: it could only have been he. The ruckus surrounding the performance had excited him tremendously. He had gone into the theater revolver in hand and spoke of firing on the audience. To tell the truth, Apollinaire's "surrealist drama" was not much to his liking; he deemed the play too literary and strongly disapproved of the costume design.

As we went out, he confided that he wasn't alone in Paris. The evening before, leaving La Pitié after hoping to find me there, he had gone for a walk and, near the Gare de Lyon, had been *fortunate enough* to rescue a "little girl" from two thugs who were manhandling her. He had taken the child under his wing; she couldn't have been more than sixteen or seventeen. What was she doing, hanging around a train station in the middle of the night? He hadn't worried about it. Because she seemed extremely tired, he had offered to take her on the train, it didn't matter where, and thus they ended up in Fontenay-aux-Roses. There they had begun to walk, and it was only at Jeanne's insistence that he had finally sought shelter for the night. It was now around four o'clock. A man putting out the streetlamps, who by a poetic coincidence was an undertaker by day, offered them hospitality. The next day—the day of our appointment—they had gotten up late and had barely made it back to Montmartre in time. Jacques had asked the girl to wait for him in a grocery store with a few pennies' worth of candy. He was leaving me at the end of the afternoon to go join her. She was very young, apparently rather naive; he had slung his staff officer's ID card around her neck. She accompanied us to the Rat Mort, where Jacques Vaché showed me a few of his war sketches, notably some studies for a "Lafcadio." He obviously felt great tenderness for Jeanne and had promised to take her to Biarritz; in the meantime he was staying with her in a hotel near the Bastille. Needless to say, he left by himself the next day without any more of a backward glance than usual, perfectly heedless of the sacrifice that Jeanne claimed to have made for him of her life . . . and of two days on the job. I have reason to believe that in exchange she gave him a dose of syphilis.

Three months later Jacques was again in Paris. He came to see me but soon left on that beautiful morning to go walk alone by the Ourcq canal. I can still see the long traveling coat draped over his shoulders, the somber air with which he spoke of *success in the grocery business.* "You'll think I'm missing, or dead, and one day—anything's possible—" (he uttered this sort of expression in a singsong voice) "you'll learn that a certain Jacques Vaché is living in retirement in some Normandy or other. He spends his time raising livestock. He'll introduce you to his wife, a rather pretty and innocent young thing, who will never suspect the danger she was courting. Only a few books—very few, mind you—carefully locked away on the top floor will bear witness to the fact that something happened." Even this illusion would soon abandon him, as attested by his letter of 9 May 1918.

The last stage of Jacques Vaché's life is marked by his famous letter of 14 November, which all my friends know by heart: "I'll emerge from the war gently doddering, perhaps indeed like those splendid village idiots (and I hope so) . . . or else . . . or else . . . what a film I'll play in!—With insane automobiles, don't you know, and bridges that collapse, and enormous hands creeping

over the screen toward some document—useless and priceless!—
With such tragic conversations, in evening wear," etc.; and this
delirium, more poignant for us than the deliria of *A Season in
Hell:* "I'll also be a trapper, or thief, or prospector, or hunter, or
miner, or well driller. Arizona Bar (whiskey, gin and mixed) and
fine, high-yielding forests, and you know those beautiful riding
breeches with their machine pistols, the clean-shaven look, and
such lovely hands for playing solitaire. It'll all go up in smoke, I
tell you, or in a saloon, having made my fortune.—Well."

Jacques Vaché killed himself in Nantes shortly after the armis-
tice. His death was admirable in that it could pass for an accident.
I believe he absorbed forty grams of opium, although, as you
might well imagine, he was not an inexperienced smoker. On the
other hand, it is quite possible that his unfortunate companions
did not know how to use drugs and that he wanted, in disappearing, to play a final *hilarious trick* on them.

I do not make a practice of honoring the dead, but this existence
that I was pleased and displeased to retrace here is, you can be
sure, practically the only thing that still binds me to a dimly fore-
seeable future and to some minor problems. All the literary or
artistic cases that I'm forced to consider take their place behind
him, and even then they hold my attention only insofar as I can
measure their human significance against this infinite scale. This is
why everything that can be *accomplished* in the intellectual domain
will always smack for me of the worst servility or the sheerest bad
faith. Naturally I like only things that are unfinished, and have no
fonder wish than to take on too much. Any embrace, any pure
domination, is a trap. And it is enough, for the moment, that
such a pretty shadow should be dancing on the ledge of the window out of which, each day, I will hurl myself again and again.

Guillaume Apollinaire

Many years from now those of us who have reached sufficient age to have memories imposed on us will speak of Guillaume Apollinaire. To have known him will be considered a rare privilege. Young people will rediscover the artless expression "I came too late." The rest of us will preserve the poet's image, having kept it intact through our great love.

Still, how many of us have already recognized our souls in:

> *the troop of women*
> *Who came out of the houses*
> *Who came out of the side streets with wild eyes*
> *Their hands stretched out toward the melodious seducer*

In all the beings who rouse our emotions, following their destiny of cruelty:

> *He strolled along indifferently playing his tune*
> *He strolled along so terribly* [1]

Since "The Pont Mirabeau" Apollinaire has been strolling along before us in the same way. As with certain birds in the Middle Ages, the soul of ancient Sirens seems to be reincarnated in him. He is practically the only living poet who can cry out, "I am the richest a thousand times over,"

> *I who know sad lays for queens*
> *The ballads of regretful years*
> *The choruses of sea-doomed slaves*
> *The romance of the poorly-loved*
> *And songs which only sirens sing*

1. "The Musician of Saint-Merry."

Back before the war. Let's dry our eyes. Genius is reborn, all the more beautiful, from the burning bouquet of catastrophe. The poet's resurrection ushers in a troubled epoch.

The new Lazarus shook himself like a wet dog and left the cemetery. It was three o'clock in the afternoon and bills relating to the mobilization were posted everywhere.

We have seen *Les Soirées de Paris* and *Le Festin d'Esope* try on madeira-colored gowns. Beneath this rotting exterior, like a luscious fruit, Apollinaire's art ran the risk, perhaps, of spoiling.

A splendid collection of meteors, *Calligrammes* is marked by the firmament of war. Gladiolus-rockets; explosions like muslin roses. I draw the reader's gaze to this poetic transmutation:

APRIL NIGHT 1915

The sky is starred by the Boche's shells
The marvelous forest where I live is giving a ball
The machinegun plays a tune in three-fourths time
But have you the word
Eh! yes the fatal word
To the battlements To the battlements Leave the picks there

Like a star frantically seeking its seasons
Heart exploded shell you whistled your love song
And your thousand suns have emptied the caissons
That the gods of my eyes fill in silence

We love you oh life and we get on your nerves
The shells whined a love unto death
A dying love is sweeter than others
Your breath swims the river where blood will run dry
Shells were whining
    Hear our shells sing
Their deep-purple love hailed by our men going to die

The wet springtime the night light the attack

It's raining my soul it's raining but it's raining dead eyes

Ulysses how many days to get back to Ithaca

Lie down in the straw and dream a fine remorse
Which as a pure effect of art is aphrodisiac

But

　　organ music
　　among the straw whisps where you slumber
The hymn of the future is paradisiac

Only the greatest poets can always cause "a bit of straw in the stable" to shine.

Apollinaire, who refused to see anything as pernicious, took it on himself to ponder the spectacles of war without bitterness. No surprise, then, to see him extoll military life: at least it was new, and all the more tolerable in that he had chosen it himself. The thought that Guillaume Apollinaire was firing a cannon in Nîmes showed me just how great the upheaval was.

Dull barracks life did not bother him. For his poetry, there were horses to name, new relationships, and street signs. And above all, there was the hope of a better tomorrow.

The supreme force is desire

and I do not consider any of this a constraint. Let us instead grant the poet a phenomenal gift of wonder. He is the same one who, on Boulevard de Montmorency, expected colored pencils and Dutch candy from Jean Royère.[2]

Oh God how lovely war is
With its songs its long leisures

in joy as well as in pain:

2. The reference is taken from Apollinaire's letter to Breton of 2 August 1916, in which he complains of not having heard from Symbolist poet Royère since he "brought me Dutch candies and colored pencils while I was at Villa Molière." Apollinaire had been hospitalized at Villa Molière earlier that year for treatment of a head wound. (trans.)

We're doing fine but the grocery car which they say is marvelous doesn't come this far.

One of the most moving pages of this book is the one about

THE BLEEDING-HEART DOVE AND THE FOUNTAIN

—in other words, love and friendship. I will not try to justify its typographic layout to those who expect poets to account for their whims. I've read in *La Papesse Jeanne* that the Gauls arranged their Bacchic songs in the shape of a barrel. Personally, I regret that "L'Horloge de Demain," from the magazine *391,* could not be reprinted in *Calligrammes.* I believe that this work, while remaining within the popular tradition of graffiti, on the border between the art of writing and the art of painting, inaugurates a whole series of experiments. There are plenty of other readers who will prefer "Lou," "Honor's Hymn," or "Sorrow of a Star."

The poet has made his annunciation. He has revived those gods whose death he once deplored: the great Pan, or Love. Let us not forget to honor him for it, the moment they return.

> *This is the time of magic*
> *It's coming back You may expect*
> *Billions of wonders*
> *Listen to the stilled oracles being reborn*

The order in which these poems appear is not accidental. Just consider the book's various parts: "Waves," "Banners," "Flutchel," "Flash of Gunfire," "Moon-Colored Shells," "The Starry Head." Couldn't we see in them variations familiar to the soul of every warrior, leading from singing departures to glorious halt? In a painting by Henri Rousseau, the older the Douanier's progeny get, the gentler their gazes. The grandfather's is totally lacking in malice. Did he have nothing other to do than be pleased with his good life? What a joy to discover such implications in the poets.

The author of *Calligrammes,* "free of any ties, detached," so he claims, "from all natural things," makes us share in his magnificent self-assurance:

> *I tell you what life really is*
> *Only I could sing this way*
> *My songs are scattering like seeds*
> *Hush all you others who sing*
> *Don't mix your darnel with my grain*

either by making us fear for his life or by presenting himself as a creature of legend:

> *Did you know Galloping Guy*
> *In the days when he was a soldier*
> *Did you know Galloping Guy*
> *When he was an artilleryman*
> *During the war*

> *I bequeath to the future the story of Guillaume Apollinaire*
> *Who was in the war and knew how to be everywhere*

The chapbook that appeared under the title *Vitam Impendere Amori*[3] gave no hint of such outpourings. Its landscape made of canvases and its few theatrical affectations fortunately kept us from seeing it as Guillaume Apollinaire's answer to *La Partenza*. It is on the stage, when the light is just dim enough, that the poet—who is a bit too susceptible to Italian *commedia dell'arte*—modulates his complaint to the tinkling of little bells.

As a teller of tales Apollinaire distills his "*phials of phantasy*" in dazzling colored beakers. The style of *The Heresiarch and Co.* (1910) is itself "adorned with smutty, almost obscene words, which are nevertheless startlingly expressive. It is a habit of mystics to use such words, for mysticism often verges on eroticism."

Apollinaire has vowed always to satisfy the Desire for the unexpected, the sign of modern tastes. Already one of Jarry's characters would shoot at the bell with a pistol from where he sits, just to summon you.[4] We know how Lafcadio fixed it so that the door happened to give way when his fellow traveler leaned on

3. With drawings by André Rouveyre.
4. *The Supermale.*

it.[5] Is there any sign of the times more remarkable than the current war? In all lucidity, I can see how urgent such distractions have become to twentieth-century man. The pleasure they give us, according to my friend Jacques Vaché, is linked to the sense we have of their theatrical Pointlessness.

At the same time, we are drawn by exhorbitantly luxurious creatures: take as proof the physical appearance of the Supermale, or André Derain's portrait of *Chevalier X.*

We have made a success of paradoxical Emotional Responses: Ubu and the bear, the Little Tramp.[6] And the notion of something UBU-ically tremendous counts for a great deal in our terrible joy.

Our tastes (for inexplicable facts, etc.) are more or less those of Clarisse, Paul Morand's mysterious and beautiful heroine:[7]

Small, unimaginable, ageless objects, never even dreamed of: the museum of a wild child, curiosities from insane asylums, the collection of some consul made anemic by the tropics . . . broken mechanical toys, burnt milk, steam organs, the smell of priests, black silk corsets with stays, and colored pearl bouquets made of all the flowers cited in Shakespeare . . .

And I am suddenly reminded of the deliria of *A Season in Hell:*

I loved absurd paintings, door panels, stage sets, backdrops for acrobats, signboards . . .

More than the object, she loves its imitation. . . . She loves this paraphrase of authenticity, the modern religion of the trompe-l'oeil, and the latent mockery of the false object. . . . To dress up in

5. André Gide, *Lafcadio's Adventures.* [In this original instance of the *acte gratuit,* Gide's eponymous hero causes his traveling companion, a total stranger, to fall out of the train to his death.—trans.]

6. "A vaudeville sign erected its horrors before me" (Rimbaud). [In the next sentence, the phrase "UBU-ically tremendous" comes from Jacques Vaché's letter to Breton of 29 April 1917.—trans.].

7. "Clarisse ou l'Amitié," in *Le Mercure de France* (16 May 1917).

drag is one of her joys. She makes up her materials, dyes her rugs, bleaches her hair, paints her cats. A thousand objects surround her, each destined for uses other than the ones you would suppose.

One of Apollinaire's characters, moreover, dismisses our passions in a few words:

I'm telling you, I saw your woman. She is ugliness and beauty; she is like everything we love today.[8]

The poets know, they who are fluent in the language of the heart.

The unexpected that beckons us results at times from the situation (Rimbaud as a carnival barker in Stockholm), at times from a risky literary effect. Apollinaire came up with quite a few of these:

I was walking in the country with a charming chimney who had her dog on a leash

We cannot stand the light in certain scenes of the *Heresiarch*: that of the lightning in "Simon Magus," the harsh daylight in "Cox City." The title of the book, along with four or five of the stories,[9] imposes a fog that is indistinct from theological quarrels. But the greatest mastery is reached in "Que Vlo-ve?" in which supernaturalism finds its tongue.

Que Vlo-ve? was the divinity of that forest in which Geneviève de Brabant wandered, from the banks of the Meuse to the Rhine, past Eiffel, that ancient volcano, whose dead seas are called the ponds of Daun; that Eiffel from which gushes the spring of Saint-Apollinaire, and the lake of the Maria Laach, which is a pool of the virgin's spittle.

One of the first lines of Poe's "Ulalume," as translated into French by Mallarmé, perfectly captures that music—like gold pebbles rolled in a torrent. The poet of *Alcools* (1913) excels in the delicate play of alliteration:

8. Cf. Baudelaire, "The Soup and the Clouds."
9. Among them, "The Latin Jew," "The Heresiarch," and "Infallibility."

Comme la vie est lente
Et comme l'Espérance est violente

[How slow life seems to me
How violent the hope of love can be]

Moreover, his fabulous knowledge of prosody has stopped being laudable. Not content with being an innovator in the field of expression, he sought to infuse poetic technique with his art. And so, even while accepting the distinction between "masculine" and "feminine" rhymes, he tries to redefine their gender.[10] He is in fact attacking the *arbitrariness* of this distinction, since no one is less inclined than he to cast off its charming yoke.

From the opening lines of "The Song of the Poorly Loved," doesn't he unmistakably invoke Villon? I listen with pleasure to Fernand Fleuret:

The poetry of Guillaume Apollinaire is rural, like that of François the student. Here, bars replace taverns; the waiting areas of train stations, with their scum and miserable emigrants, replace the sordid squares of ancient Paris. The poetic commonplaces dear to Deschamps, Villon, Marot—such as chance loves, laborious destiny, nostalgia for youth, the fleeting passage of time, sterile indolence, and Death—account for the best of Alcools*'s inspiration. And I rediscover in Guillaume Apollinaire the great French poet's contradictory emotions, which it would be impossible, even for the most resolutely bookish mind, to simulate for two hundred pages. Like Villon, he laughs through his tears; he is profligate and an easy prey, realistic and refined, skeptical and credulous, virile and weak. He is the people of Paris, the People itself.*

Among so many poems I could cite—"1909," "Autumn Rhénane," "Twilight," "Marizibill"—I must single out, from all this perfection,

10. "The Hermit," in *Alcools.*

20 *Guillaume Apollinaire*

THE CROCUSES

The meadow is deadly though fair in autumn
Cows grazing there
Slowly are poisoned

There crocuses color of eye-ring color of lilac
Bloom   your eyes like these flowers
Like their rings and like autumn are violet
My life from your eyes slowly takes poison

Schoolchildren noisily come
Wearing jackets playing harmonicas
To pick crocuses that are like mothers
Daughters of their daughters they are the color of your eyelids
Fluttering like flowers in a crazy wind

Softly the cowherd sings
While cows slow and lowing abandon
Forever meadows so evilly flowered by autumn

This little work counts among the book's lyric masterpieces.
Apollinaire has also included "The Thief" and "The Emigrant
from Landor Road," which is his "Drunken Boat." From the
former I excerpt, in defense of the alexandrine, the stanzas

Fruit rounded like souls lay scattered
And pinecone almonds littered
Your sea garden where I posed my oars
And left my Punic knife beneath the peach tree

Oil-tinted lemons tasting of cool water
Swayed among the blossoms of the twisted grove
The birds have pecked your pomegranates
And nearly all the figs were split

. . . .
Porridge grown cold will seem dull to your lips
But a goatskin bottle keeps the white wine chill
Do you wish them ironically to serve a dish of beans
Or fritters of flowers dipped in blond honey

But the poet owed it to himself to carry out his own assassination. One day he simply abandoned his joyous heritage and set off on the road to discovery.

Then he sternly questioned the universe. He became accustomed to the immense light of depths. And sometimes he consented to use actual objects: a twopenny song, an authentic postage stamp.[11]

He even uttered this beautiful cry of discouragement:

Compete then poet with the labels of perfume bottles

Beginning with "Monday on Rue Christine," there was no longer any point in criticizing the successive formulas through which his research attained its goals. There was no turning Guillaume Apollinaire away from his true aim: the reinvention of poetry.

> *Lose*
> *But lose genuinely*
> *To make room for discovery*

Some have spoken of incoherence, and how constantly blind fate sways our emotions! These reflections are touching only because their disorder has psychological truth:

> *One evening I stopped at a dreary inn*
> *Near the Luxembourg*
> *In the depth of the room a Christ was soaring*
> *Someone had a ferret*
> *Another a hedgehog*
> *We played cards*
> *And you you had forgotten me*

The singular power of the poem "Zone" is established along the same lines.

Apollinaire, pilot of the heart, let us simply navigate. I think back to the feelings one can have on first discovering such pages:

11. "Picasso," in *The Cubist Painters.*

*These unloved children understand so much! Oh mother,
please love me!*

*These unloved women remember. They've repeated their
brittle ideas too many times today.*[12]

*In the prow of the boat that I was steering
A dead man spoke with a young woman
Who wore a yellow dress
A black blouse
With blue ribbons and a grey hat
Adorned with one small uncurling feather*[13]

Women's shoes left by the bed expressed a tender haste.[14]

It was with the same spirit that Guillaume Apollinaire wrote
art criticism. Above all, perhaps, his "aesthetic meditations" on
The Cubist Painters display his extreme sensitivity. Doesn't his
"Picasso" still throb with life?

Always curious about things not yet experienced, the poet
flies alongside the latest trends. "*I,*" he says, "*am not afraid of
art.*" In this we have the best proof of his courage, until the blaze
snatches him away.

It's a pleasure to watch him make our cautious tastes more adventurous:

*We don't love intensely enough the joy
Of seeing beautiful new things
   Oh my dear make haste
Be afraid that someday a train will no longer thrill you
   Look at it faster for your own sake*

And it is also to his credit that he fought so hard to impose
the wonderful talents of certain painters. Apart from Picasso,
the dearest among them include Marie Laurencin, André Derain,
Georges Braque, Giorgio de Chirico, Francis Picabia, Marcel

12. Ibid.
13. "The House of the Dead."
14. "Picasso," in *The Cubist Painters.*

Duchamp, and Marc Chagall. The calligramatic prefaces to the catalog for the Léopold Survage and Irène Lagut exhibit are yesterday's games. Apollinaire managed to make us love the "poor old angel" who was Henri Rousseau. Earlier he was among the first to turn toward Henri Matisse.

Delaunay can elegantly claim this statement from the "Aesthetic Meditations" to his credit:

> *I love today's art, because I love light above all and every man loves light above all, for man invented fire.*

And *The Poet Assassinated* glows beneath the colorless rush of its cover. The book went to press before the war. Its story is pathetic. Love and life are heart-rendingly mocked: the Baron des Ygrées died gallantly out of desire for Mia, and a few days later the young woman "sold her virginity to a millionaire crack skeet shooter." It was even the thirty-fifth time that she had indulged "in that little commercial operation"!

Apollinaire has said apropos of Giorgio de Chirico that "in depicting the fatal character of modern things, surprise is the most modern resource at our disposal." *The Poet Assassinated* is like the defense and illustration of this principle. The chapter entitled "Fashion" and the plot of *Ieximal Jelimite* carry the day.

Harpooning the monster of the down-to-earth, the poet frees a charming Andromeda: imagination. She governs the course of the book, which goes from narrative to dialogue, from lyricism to caricature. The book recognizes no obligation to be chronological. Its asides make it more playful still.

Eroticism casts enormous lights over the work:

> *Oh, the beautiful and unbending phalli which these cannon are! If women had had to do military service, they would have joined the artillery. The sight of cannon must be strange during a battle.*

The book's autobiographical value adds to its interest. The poet first relives, with great candor, the unforgettable sensations of his childhood. We witness his very personal education. Among those who contributed to it were Petrarch, Villon, Ronsard, Racine, and La Fontaine, as well as Perrault, and Lamartine with *La Chute d'un ange.* He read Sade and the bawdy authors of the eighteenth century: Laclos, Nerciat, Restif de la Bretonne; chivalric novels; the Robinsons; popular novels and specialized works: catalogs, medical journals, travel narratives, linguistics and grammar texts, American epics in installments.

Still, there was one precept he never abandoned:

Learn all about nature and love it.

The Poet Assassinated captivates me all the more in that I can identify its principal actors. The Bird of Benin signed, as Picasso, infinitely moving canvases. Tristouse Ballerinette is just as graceful under her real name;[15] it was she who, in other times, calling herself Viviane or the Lady of the Lake, enchanted Merlin. And so she had already come to dance on the grave of the enchanter whose death she had caused.

If *Bestiary or The Parade of Orpheus,* in the context of Apollinaire's work, is no more than an amusement, I would still almost dare say, "love and Sirens still sing so harmoniously there that the very life of whoever hears them is not too high a price to pay for such music." Never under Mallarmé did the French stanza know such limpidity. I wonder, then, whether we truly needed to see, as Apollinaire claims, the drawings that accompany this cry articulated in the shadows, "which seemed to be the voice of light"[16]—even if these drawings are by Dufy, whose woodcut images, to my mind, are but a useless decoration of the poem, no more or less appropriate than Raffaelli's earlier illustrations for Mallarmé's "street types":

15. The character was based on Apollinaire's lover, the painter Marie Laurencin. (trans.)

16. The *Pimander.*

THE DOVE

Dove, the love and the spirit
That gave birth to Jesus,
Like you I love a Mary,
Please God that we may marry.

THE SIRENS

Sirens, do I understand your distress,
As you lament offshore in the night?
I am like you, sea, full of subtle cries;
My singing ships are called the years.

THE ELEPHANT

Like an elephant with his ivory,
I hold a treasure in my mouth.
Purple death! . . . I buy my fame
With sweetly singing words.

Seven years later *Les Mamelles de Tirésias* appeared in book form.
How can this "surrealist drama," performed for the first time
on 24 June 1917, rekindle all those old hatreds in this day and
age: "fiery hatreds of old against young, of young against old, of
young against young," which, as Madame Rachilde tells us, were
declared on the occasion of *Ubu Rex*? If not for this, the critics
would never have thought of drawing a parallel between these
two plays. Just as weakly, the names of Aristophanes and Rabe-
lais were brought up. Without prejudice to its satiric and moral
import, I would say that, if one had to relate Apollinaire's work
to someone else's, it should be to John Millington Synge's *Play-
boy of the Western World,* about which the author of *Mamelles* has
himself said, "Such strong poetry, of a constantly unexpected perfection, emanates from its realism that I'm not surprised people
found it shocking." *Les Mamelles de Tirésias* seems to me a good-
natured play, which I found it restful to laugh at unself-con-
sciously. I know that Apollinaire holds the key to a modern gaiety,

which is both more profound and more tragic than this, and that he purposely did not bring it forth here.

I prefer to say that the play, in its choice of means, does not boast the same infallibility as Jarry's masterpiece. Nonetheless, it does reexamine the New Spirit, whose immense corpus weighed on Apollinaire.

One can love certain individuals to the point of not wanting to imagine their futures, and so I will refrain from speaking here of *The Rotting Enchanter*[17] as Guillaume Apollinaire's future. It also seems premature for me to deflower the "adorable spring-time" after I've taken pains to depict Guillaume Apollinaire only as he appeared to me when I was twenty.[18]

Some will say I have not ventured very far in exploring Apollinaire's soul. I can reply only that if the enchanter had revealed all his secrets to me, I would already have enclosed him in a magic circle and put him in the tomb. And so I would like the gaps in my knowledge to stand as a measure of the prestige he still enjoys in my eyes.

1917

17. 1909, with woodcuts by André Derain.

18. The irony of the remark is that Breton was barely twenty-one when he wrote these lines. A further irony, in the following paragraph, is that Apollinaire went "in the tomb" within weeks of the article's first publication. (trans.)

Alfred Jarry

Alfred Jarry expected to become a solemn, portly gentleman and, as mayor of some small town, to receive vases in Sèvres porcelain as gifts from the local fire marshal. I am one of those young people who would one day have reviled him. If I now come, after—and before—others who are more qualified than I, to pay homage to his memory, it is because the features with which I picture him (I who never knew the man) seem to be absolutely indelible. I believe I can judge his work with sufficient objectivity. The man himself seems detached from the worst conditions of his existence. I have no personal recollections with which to pad this. We must recognize that the lesson of our era is tending to set us, with respect to Jarry, on the road to restitution. We who reached our twentieth year—that is, the age at which one begins to determine one's life—during the current war were forced, by this very fact, to confront some implacable realities. So as to avoid a certain displeasure, we chose to attach very little importance to anything. We began to require a similar sacrifice from our poets and philosophers. None proved better able to resist such an assault on what was reasonable than did Jarry.

The author of *Ubu Rex* did not yet have a biography, properly speaking. We know that he was born in Laval in 1873—on 8 September, to be exact, the day of the Virgin's nativity. As a child he might have been taken a few times to the pilgrimage of Saint Anne, for he later remembered "a host of things he saw there, and that had never been." Once he confided to us that his hero Sengle was very fond of swamps: "You never know what creatures you'll find there, nor even, what with the sun drying them out, whether you'll find the same swamp, or any swamp at all, and it will always seem as if you've dreamed them up." Moreover, here is the sonnet in which he re-creates his world of that time:

The pubic arch of menhirs straddles the moor,
The deaf-mute prowls, hand stretched for a tip,
Around the pit where lie the martyrs' bones,
Lowering his groping lantern from a string.

Over the carmine waves the wind's horn blows.
The sea-unicorn sways through the barren heath.
The shadow of bony ghosts lit by the moon
Glints steel-like on the sable and the ermine.

The man-shaped oak has known that shadow's smile.
C'havann, the owl, eating the whirr of may-bugs,
Perches, a ruffled sea-urchin, on a far rock.

The traveler's footsteps write upon his shadow.
Not waiting for the sky to strike midnight,
The stone re-echoes from the feathers' strokes.

Alfred Jarry attended the lycée in Rennes. How, from the dreamy young man he was when he started, did he become the jaded adult he seems to be at age fifteen (around 1888 *Ubu Rex* was playing at the Théâtre des Phynances)? He must have suffered some very cruel injustices early on. It is clear that his life was poisoned like no one else's. Taking his physics teacher as model, he conceived in Ubu a creature of ugliness, stupidity, and pettiness. Who, in his entire life, will emerge from that fellow's shadow? Later it was in these terms that Jarry suggested liquidating him:

He is not entirely Mr. Thiers, nor the bourgeois, nor the boor. Rather, he would be the perfect anarchist, except for what prevents us from ever becoming perfect anarchists: that he is a man, whence cowardice, filth, and so on.

Of the three souls distinguished by Plato: the head, the heart, and the strumpot, only this last is not embryonic in him.

I do not know what the name Ubu means; it is the more eternal deformation of the name of his inadvertent and still-living

*prototype: Ybex, perhaps, the Vulture. But this is only one scene
of the role he plays.*

*If he resembles an animal, he particularly has a porcine face,
a nose similar to the crocodile's upper jaw, and the totality of
his cardboard caparison makes him overall brother to the most
aesthetically horrible of all marine beasts, the sea louse.*

In Paris, in 1893, Jarry contributed to *L'Art littéraire,* in which
he notably published his first poem, "The Dead Man's Lullaby
for Going to Sleep." He was under the influence of Mallarmé, as
can be seen in parts of *Minutes de Sable Mémorial,* published the
following year. Over the lintel of this book appears this cerebral
blindman's buff: "Suggest instead of saying; in the path of sentences, make every word a crossroads." On Rue de Rome[1] he
would stop seeing things as accidental. On the other hand, he
derived great pleasure from irritating his guests. In order to get
to his home on Boulevard de Port-Royal, one had to squeeze
through a narrow dead-end alleyway that led to a place called
"Dead Man's Calvary." Scenery out of *Haldernablou* found a second home in his. Left-hand wall: on a white stove, in a recess, a
monumental sculpted death's head; a bed with a reliquary above
it, a Madonna in the corner. In back the crossbars of the window
closed off by a curtain and a table. Right-hand wall: the door,
section of bare wall with a fencing glove exhuming three fingers
from the shadows, a fencing foil, a pistol; a mirror facing the recess, lamp on the table, both very low. The stench from the owl
cage could easily prove discomfiting. The walls of the stairwell re-
tain bloody handprints.

One is no more at ease in the *Minutes.* The principal sensations
registered by sight, hearing, and touch are dullness and viscosity.
The poet extolls the mandrake, no doubt because of its fleshy,
bifurcated root, reminiscent of a human trunk and its two legs.
For companions he gives himself the bat with its hourly flight and

1. In the 1890s Jarry frequented Mallarmé's Tuesday gatherings in his Rue
de Rome apartment. (trans.)

the nightjar, the chameleon, the trapdoor spider. Then, having re-moved one by one the sleeves of his earthly body, he takes on the form of Mr. Ubu (paunch, suitcase, cap, umbrella). On his orders "the hirsute trinity of Palcontents flies out in a phallic spurt" from his three oxblood-colored traveling trunks. "With beards of white, red, and black, with Phyrigian muddergoose coifs,[2] wrapped in versicolored jerkins, they wave their placid arms, which cross over their ringed caterpillar bodies" and "make their diabolic, quiver-ing ears stand up like antennae." Carrying green torches, they intone this hymn in their squeaky voices:

> *Brothers, light up the way of your lord — fat pilgrim — we fol-low him on, joyful no doubt: in giant tin boxes shut up the whole week long. Only on Sunday do we breathe fresh air, grooms of the Serpents of Bronze in their lair: we are the Pals, we are the Cons, we are the Palcontents.*
>
> *Ears to the wind, in closest ranks, we march warlike and scary, and people who see us passing by think we're the military.*
>
> *We are the Palcontents! We get our eats through platinum teats, we pee through a tap without a handle. And we inhale the atmostale through a tube as bent as a Dutchman's candle! We are the Palcontents!*

At the lycée they compliantly studied mathematics with Mr. Achras, who raised polyhedra. This Mr. Achras seems to have determined one of Jarry's vocations: won't we see him dabbling more and more in "pataphysics," or the science of imaginary solu-tions? "From the dispute between the Plus sign and the Minus sign, the Reverend Pa Ubu, of the Company of Jesus, former King of Poland, will soon write a great book entitled *Caesar Anti-christ,* in which one will find the only practical demonstration, by means of a mechanical engine called a physics rod, of the identity of opposites." Such is, in fact, the state of Jarry's faith: what can one believe in? The dead speak, return. What we call skepticism is

2. In French, *de merdoie,* a pun on *mère l'oie* (mother goose) and *merde d'oie* (goose shit). (trans.)

only bourgeois credulity. "I believe in it," he says of absolute love, "because it is absurd, as is my belief in God." In the same vein: "As the sensory organs are a cause of error, the scientific instrument amplifies sense in the direction of error." Therefore, superstition is just as valid as science. "Universal consent is already a quite miraculous and incomprehensible prejudice." And thus *Caesar Antichrist* has "places in which everything goes by blason, and certain characters are double." When the book came out (1895), Jarry, at Remy de Gourmont's behest, left *L'Art littéraire* to found *L'Ymagier*. He would console himself for the ruinous failure of this publication by founding *Perhinderion,* a magazine of prints (1896; two issues). But suddenly fame would be handed to him. When *Ubu Rex* was performed at the Théâtre de l'Oeuvre, its au-thor suddenly cut the figure of a modern and aristocratic Père Duchesne.

At the end of that memorable evening when they saw "doors open onto snowy plains under a blue sky, mantels decorated with pendulum clocks split apart to serve as doors, and palm trees grow at the feet of beds so that little elephants perched on the shelves could graze on them," Alfred Jarry already no longer owned his big marionnette. "It happened, for his penance," says Madame Rachilde, "that the puppet called Ubu began to walk all alone. It climbed out of its box, found its way into everyday parlance, into show stoppers, into the news at hand, into the highest Parisian circles, spread into the makeup and perfumes of bedroom literature. It excited Lorrain and set Mendès dreaming. The *word* showed up everywhere,[3] sprouted wings. Rochefort crowned it with a political commentary; the artists Forain and Couturier reproduced it, with or without its mask. Ubu as a type became legendary."

If it had not been for Marcel Schwob, Jarry might well have underestimated the value of his creation. The father of Monelle was the first to see it as a sign of the times. The public had

3. A reference to the celebrated opening of *Ubu Rex:* "Merdre!" commonly translated as "Pschitt!" or "Shite!" (trans.)

grown angry, not liking to have someone take serious jabs at it. "It would have been easy," Jarry said, "to tailor Ubu to the tastes of the Parisian public, by making the following minor changes: the first word would have been 'Darn' (or 'Pdarn'), the 'unspeakable brush' a young girl going to bed, the army uniforms from the First Empire; Ubu would have knighted the czar and various persons would have been cuckolded—but the whole thing would have been filthier." They did not know that Lugné-Poe intended to play the part as a tragedy; some deplored the absence of witticisms. In general the public, invited to come see its "ignoble twin," preferred to take from the play a moral of abuse. Firmly convinced of the identity of opposites, the author converted to his hero's religion. *Days and Nights* (1897), *L'Amour en visites* (1898), *L'Amour absolu* (1899), *Ubu Enchained* (1900), and *Ubu's Almanac* (1900 and 1901) are battles that he fought with an eye toward this victory over himself. (Let us recall that Sengle "had dulcinified or deified his strength.") Even in his friends' eyes,

As into himself finally eternity changes him,

from now on Jarry incarnates Pa Ubu.

THE ROYAL TOILET

Mercurial dragon rampant, charging the fess,
The Vistula's argent glister swamps the vert field.
Poland's monarch (once Aragon's) starts to undress
For the bathtub—omnipotent boob, proudly peeled!

Charlemagne had twelve years: Ubu's paragonless.
When he walks, his grease quakes; if he breathes, earth will yield:
Pa Ubu's patagonian footfalls impress
In the sand, with each toe, sable pumps—soled and heeled.

He sets forth, all escutcheoned with belly—it comes
On ahead. His redounding illustrious bum's
Breadth outstrips his poor underpants where we may meet,

Limited in genuine gold, large as life: totem-wise
On the warpath, a galloping Redskin (the seat);
The whole of the Eiffel Tower (straight up the flies).

Having decided to rely on his supernatural exterior to fashion his writings, he meanwhile recalled having been a soldier. He has said how he reacted. Sengle, in *Days and Nights,* listens to "the cook filtering the morning coffee through an obscene song" and endures the noise of washhouses, the "mom-and-pop" drumming school behind the hedges, the way of pissing. Seeing the barracks floor sprinkled "with infinity signs," he soon loses all concept of time and pledges allegiance to the Old Man of the Mountain.

The other works mentioned earlier constitute, to my mind, Ubu's paralipomena, along with two earlier plays, *Prophaiseur de Pfuisic* and *Les Polyèdres,* from which I extract the delectable

Scene of the Cobbler

CYTOTOMILLE, MONCRIF, ACHRAS

MONCRIF: *Master Cobbler, the woolidogs having stripped my feet bare of their envelopes, I beg some shoes from you.*

SCYTOTOMILLE: *Here's an excellent article, Sir, speciality of the firm—the Turd-Cruncher. For just as no two turds are alike, so does a Turd-Cruncher exist for every taste. These are for while they are still steaming; these are for horse dung; these are for the innocent meconium of a breast-fed baby; here's something for policemen's droppings; these are for ancient spyrata; and this pair here is for the stools of a middle-aged man.*

MONCRIF: *Ah, Sir! I'll take those, they'll do me very well. How much do you charge for them, Master Cobbler?*

SCYTOTOMILLE: *Fourteen francs, since you seem a respectable gentleman.*

ACHRAS: *You're making a mistake, look you, not to take this pair, look you, for policemen's droppings.*

MONCRIF: *You're quite right, Sir. Master Cobbler, I'll take the other pair.* (He starts to go.)

SCYTOTOMILLE: *But you haven't paid for them, Sir!*

MONCRIF: *Because I took them instead of those, etc., for the, etc., for the middle-aged man.*
SCYTOTOMILLE: *But you haven't paid for them, either.*
ACHRAS: *Because he hasn't taken them, look you.*
SCYTOTOMILLE: *Fair enough.* (Exeunt.)

We can still find the Jarry of that period, sure of his abilities, in the dark-eyed petty bourgeois painted by Hermann-Paul. "If ever an aesthetic aroused his passion," writes Charles Doury, "it was certainly not the art of fashion. More attentive to the movements of a sentence than to the folds of a necktie, he affected a rather curious disdain in matters of dress.

"Forever draped in a frock coat and wearing cyclist's shoes, he retained his dignity, in a left-bank café, seated before a glass of absinthe or a bottle of stout, no matter what the hour—bringing even to his dissoluteness, if I may say so, a certain discipline and principle.

"He would then speak in a measured tones, pronouncing all the mute vowels and telling, in very restrained language, the most nonsensical tales, playing in real life the part of Ubu himself and seriously bragging about imaginary exploits.

"Most of the time he lived in a small house he owned on the Marne or in Paris, in a little apartment on Rue Cassette, shuttling between his two abodes, riding his bicycle day or night, even in the pouring rain.

"Furthermore, he liked to appear in sportsman's attire. He enjoyed recounting the endurance races he had completed in the shortest possible time, at a speed rivaling that of the best racers."

One day, in a yard in Corbeil, Jarry was amusing himself by uncorking champagne with pistol shots. Across the fence the owner of the house was watching over her children. As several bullets had strayed into her yard, she ran, provincially dressed, and introduced herself with much ceremony. She pointed out to the lady of the house that she had not rented the place as a rifle range, adding, in a dignified tone, that her children could fall victim to this game. "Ah!" Jarry broke in, "not to worry, Madam, we'll simply make you some more."

It's raining cats and dogs. On a bicycle, pedaling barefoot, spattered by the puddles along the towpath, Pa Ubu heads for the Coudray dam. "Where do you think you're going?" an old woman calls down from her balcony. "Have you lost your mind, riding in this weather?" "We are going to the prefecture, where we have been invited to lunch," he answers. "Never fear, Madam, we've remembered to carry our patent-leather pumps in our pocket."

When a prostitute was murdered, at the scene of the crime they discovered, among some bills from the butcher's, Alfred Jarry's calling card. He had no sooner been cleared of suspicion than he began recounting the affair at a formal salon. The embarrassed silence of his listeners only egged him on: "And what if *we* were to ask *them* why that card was dog-eared! Hornstrumpot, can you see us leaving a dog-eared card at a whorehouse?!"[4]

One evening, after the publisher of the newspaper *Le Matin,* Edwards, had lowered the gangplank of his yacht onto a landing dock next to the "Tripod," Jarry, dressed in his most informal attire, strode on deck. The ladies invited for the occasion came forward to greet him respectfully. They sat down to the banquet, during which Edwards pointed out to Pa Ubu that he had the deplorable habit of raising toasts. "That sort of thing is fine for the lower classes, my dear Jarry." "Precisely our thinking as well," replied the latter. "Cheers!"

The "Tripod" he lived in, near Corbeil, was paid for by the sales of *Messalina* (1901).

> *My own girl, mine, for they can all lay claim;*
> *Thus not a one was truly your master.*
> *Let us now sleep, and fasten the shutters:*
> *Life is enclosed, and we are at home.*

4. A dog-eared calling card meant that the visitor had come in person. (trans.)

> *It's a little high up, and here ends the world*
> *And the absolute can no more be denied;*
> *A great thing it is to come last in line,*
> *Since this day has wearied Messalina.*

The result is that the period of *The Supermale* (1902) was devoted to fishing and pistol marksmanship. Only from time to time did Pa Ubu feel the need to come to Paris, in order to "get out into the country." Understand that absinthe and billiards formed the habitual framework of his sojourns. "Nondrinkers are," he said, "sick people who are addicted to water, that poison which has been chosen from among all other substances for ablutions and washes, and which dissolves and corrodes so thoroughly that a single drop of it in a pure liquid—absinthe, for example—turns it cloudy." So alcohol enters into the composition of "Perpetual Motion Food," with which the Supermale tries to nourish or intoxicate us. The "Ten-Thousand-Mile Race," a masterpiece of sports literature, is still its least exhilarating episode. Seeing action as a means of spoiling something, we are hungry for records, and *The Supermale* is a book of records. In love, even if one can perform indefinitely, "there lies somewhere in the distance, in the series of numbers, a moment when the woman turns screaming onto herself and runs around the bedroom like—the popular expression is admirable!—like a poisoned rat." The following moment, fallen back on the bed, she allows her lover to undress her. "Her eyes were so dark as to defy every color, like dead brown leaves at the brackish bottom of the ditches of the Lurance, so that you would have thought they were two wells in the skull bored for the sheer joy of seeing the inside of the hair through them. . . . Her teeth were tiny jewels arranged in perfect order. Death had carefully drawn the two rows together, like minuscule dominoes with no dots—too childlike to know how to count—in a surprise package."

At the same time Jarry began to publish his *Théâtre Mirlitonesque,* and he finished *Exploits and Opinions of Doctor Faustroll, Pataphysician.* In the evening gatherings hosted by the magazine

La Plume, which ran excerpts from this book, he met Guillaume Apollinaire. "Alfred Jarry," the latter said some time afterward, "seemed to me the personification of a river, a young, beardless river, with the wet clothing of a drowned man. His drooping little mustache, his frock coat whose flaps floated in the breeze, his floppy shirt and cyclist's shoes, all had something soft and spongy about them. The demigod was still damp; he had appeared only a few hours earlier, had risen trembling from his streaming bed." I prefer to think that Dr. Faustroll's boat was a sieve and give credit to the earthly Tide.

On the manuscript copy, which belongs to Mr. Louis Lormel, one can read in Jarry's hand, "This book will not be published in its entirety until the author has acquired enough experience to savor all its beauties." In writing it he thought to give us the means to "reconstitute all art and all science, in other words, Everything." Schwob's phrase "Destroy, for all creation comes from destruction," is heard by the doctor who decrees the death, on the first day, of all scavengers and soldiers; on the second, of women; on the third, of small children; on the fourth, of ruminative quadrupeds; on the fifth, of all cuckolds and bailiff's clerks; on the sixth, of certain bicyclists. He is assisted in his purgative chores by the marine bishop Mendacious. This "personage abstracted from Aldrovandi's *Monsters*" can be recognized by the pleasure he takes in unhooking shop signs and posing enigmas such as: Can an old woman ever be naked? (He makes me notice that Faustroll's publisher lacked the sign for *infinity.*) "Stupidity is not his strong point."[5] I can see him conversing with Jarry about that opus translated from the English, *Popular Lectures and Addresses,* where as seriously as you please it is stated that "following the proposition of the learned Professor Cayley, a single curve drawn in chalk on a blackboard two and a half meters long can detail all the atmospheres of a season, all the cases of an epidemic, all the haggling of the hosiers of every town," and so on.

5. A paraphrase of the opening line of Paul Valéry's *An Evening with Monsieur Teste* (1896). Breton highly admired this work and later cited it as the reason for his first solicitation of Valéry in 1914. (trans.)

Faustroll is a milestone in the history of criticism. From analytical, it becomes synthetic and rises to the level of an art.

The *Speculations* appeared in *La Revue Blanche*. There was talk of gathering them under the title *The Green Candle: Some Light on the Things of These Times.* But in a letter from Laval, dated 28 May 1906, Pa Ubu let it be known that "he is quite simply exhausted (a curious end when one has written *The Supermale).* His boiler will not explode but rather fizzle out. He will cease quietly like a dying engine." While *La Revue Blanche* and *Vers et Prose* published fragments of *La Dragonne,* Jarry drew from the same subject a play, *Le Moutardier du Pape,* and *La Papesse Jeanne,* a novel that he translated from the Greek in collaboration with Dr. Saltas. It was to the latter's house that he went every evening, shod in slippers, behatted in a large fur bonnet, and draped in a torn overcoat. He carried a heavy leaded cane, and his readiness to use two revolvers was well known. He looked so fearsome that one morning Mr. Malvy, a tenant in the building, seeing him on the landing between floors, took him for a malefactor and hid in a doorway.

For all that, we should not tarnish Jarry's legend with romanticism. He "adored owls," admitted Louis Lormel, only "because they are frowned on by the stupid hordes as evil, because they sleep by day and watch by night, because their hooked beaks have an absurd and perfectly impractical shape. . . . He loved archaic traditions, strange cases, facts that defied explanation." As such, the heraldic arts had incited his passion; he appreciated the erudition of a Marcel Schwob, was jubiliant at the sight of field maneuvers: "One never tires of watching soldiers." In his reviews in *La Revue Blanche* of books on such topics as "the decisions of Judge Magnault, collected and annotated," "the gnostic tree," "the superiority of animals over man," "French grammar" (published by Le Réformiste), "golf in England and golf clubs in France," "the birth rate in France in 1900," or "the fisherman's and hunter's rulebooks," I believe I can recognize the Methods he applied to himself. On the moral plane, where had his own methods not already led him? He passed for a cynic, and it was after having apparently "broken with all his friends, as with himself," that he died in La Charité hospital, on All Saints' Day 1907.

Memnon's statue never sang more appropriately:

WALTZ

A cabinet-maker was I for many a long year . . .

1918

Jacques Vaché

The snowball centuries as they roll gather no more than humanity's tiny footsteps. One finally secures one's place in the sun only to be smothered under an animal pelt. A bonfire in the frozen countryside attracts only wolves, at best. We do not really know what premonitions are worth if these jumps in the celestial Securities Exchange, the storms that Baudelaire spoke of, sometimes make an angel appear in the spyhole.

So it was that in 1916 this poor employee on his night rounds let a butterfly land under the reflector in his desk. Despite his pretty eye shade—we were in the West—he seemed to have no more in his head than a Morse alphabet. He spent his time dreaming of the cliffs of Etretat and playing leapfrog with the clouds, and so he warmly welcomed the aviation officer. To tell the truth, we never knew in which branch of the armed forces Jacques served. I saw him plated in armor—no, plated isn't the right word: it was pure sky. He shone with a river about his neck—the Amazon, I think, which still irrigates Peru. He had burned down great parcels of virgin forest: one could tell by his hair, and by all the lovely animals that had taken refuge in him. It was not the rattlesnake that kept me from shaking his hand. More than anything, he was terrified of certain experiments in bodily distention. If, as he said, that led only to derailments! The white-hot iron bar in *Michael Strogoff* could not have blinded him. I often heard him disparage *Le Maître des forges,* which he hadn't read.[1]

"The razor's fire spreads to two or three little rooms shaped like

1. Jules Verne's *Michael Strogoff* (1876) and Georges Ohnet's *Le Maître des forges* (1882) were extremely popular works of fiction. (trans.)

eggs in a nest. You would do well to come back later. The horse-shoe is a delightful invention, to be used by sedentary people, and is explained by the verses of Alfred de Musset.—In Grecian times, the Soissons vase" (he pointed to his head, the ornament on the mantelpiece); and so on.

Male elegance steps out of the ordinary. The cover of *Miroir des modes*[2] is the color of the water bathing the skyscraper in which it is printed. Human bellies set on pilings make excellent parachutes, by the way. The smoke escaping from these top hats frames in black the honorary diploma that we wanted to show our friends and acquaintances. Someday our decorations will climb up on us like kittens.

If we still kneel before woman, it is only to tie her shoelaces. In one's inward turnings, it is best to take paved roads. Madam's carriage is advanced, since her horses are falling into the sea. Loving and being loved are happening on the pier; it's risky. Be assured that we gamble more than our fortunes in casinos. Above all, don't cheat. Do you know, Jacques, the lovely movements mistresses make on-screen, when one has *finally* lost everything? Show us your hands, in which air is the great musical instrument: too lucky, you're too lucky. Why do you so enjoy making the blue blood rush to that girl's cheeks? I once knew an apartment that was a marvelous spiderweb.

In the center of the room was a rather squat bell that made an annoying sound every year or every fifteen minutes. According to it, war had not always existed, no one had ever known what could happen these days, and so on. It was enough to make you laugh, of course. The stevedore he was at the time never missed; his girlfriend wove him beautiful debts like lace. The former student of Luc-Olivier Merson certainly knew that in France passing counterfeit bills is severely punished. What did you want us to do about it? The thrilling poster: *They're back.—Who?—The Vampires,* and in the darkened auditorium the red letters of *That same evening.* You know, I no longer need to hold onto the rail to walk

2. A lavishly produced fashion magazine of the time. (trans.)

down, and under plush soles, the stairway stops being an accordion.

We were those joyful terrorists, hardly more sentimental than was fashionable. The future is a beautiful striated leaf that takes on colorings and shows remarkable holes. It is strictly up to us to dig with both hands into fallen heads of hair. Future meals are served on an oil slick. The factory engineer and the general farmer have aged. "Our warm countries are hearts. We have led our lives briskly. — My dear André, schemata leave you cold. I had this rum brought over from Jamaica. Farming, you see, stiffens the prairie grasses; on the other hand, I'm counting on slumber to shear my sheep. The morning lark is yet another of your parables."

Equilibrium is rare. The earth that turns on its axis in twenty-four hours is not the only pole of attraction. In brilliant Colorado girls ride on horseback and superbly ravage our desire. The starry blouses of the water carriers are our related calculus. Crusaders stop to drink at poisoned wells.

The famous baptism of fire fades back into the night of adorable superstitions, in which these two fish figure for me, tied together with string. To this night I abandon you. Fruits grow moldy on the branch in the black foliage. I don't know whether the grain is being threshed or whether we should look nearby for a beehive. I am reminded of a Jewish wedding. A Dutch interior is the farthest thing there is. I can see you, Jacques, as a shepherd from the Landes: you have tall stilts made of chalk. A bushel of emotions comes cheap this year. You have to do something for a living, and the pretty relief worker with her soiled bonnet is a milkmaid in the fog. You deserved better — jail, for instance. I thought you would be with me when I went to see the first episode of *La Nouvelle Aurore* — my dearest Palas.[3] Forgive me. Ah, we're both dead!

It's true that the world manages to block all infernal machines.

3. *La Nouvelle Aurore* was a serial film by Edouard Violet, whose hero, Palas, is wrongly sentenced to death for murder. (trans.)

Isn't there any lost time? Time, you mean seven-league boots. Boxes of watercolors are decomposing. The sixteen springtimes of William R. G. Eddie[4] . . . let's keep that between ourselves.

I once knew a man more beautiful than a reed pipe. He wrote letters as serious as the Gauls. We are in the twentieth century (of the Christian era), and caps explode beneath children's heels. There are flowers that bloom in inkwells specifically for obituaries. This man was my friend.

4. An imaginary film character created by Vaché in his letter to Breton of 14 November 1918: "William R. G. Eddie, who is sixteen years old, has thousands of liveried Negroes, such beautiful ash-white hair, and a horn-rimmed monocle. He will be married." (trans.)

Two Dada Manifestoes

§I

Historical anecdotes are of little importance. It is impossible to know where and when DADA was born. The name, which one of us was happy to find for it, has the advantage of being perfectly equivocal.

Cubism was a school of painting; Futurism, a political movement: DADA is a state of mind. To compare one to the other demonstrates either ignorance or bad faith.

When it comes to religion, freethinking does not resemble a church. DADA is artistic freethinking.

So long as they make schoolchildren recite prayers in the form of book reports and museum visits, we will cry out against despotism and try to disrupt the ceremony.

DADA devotes itself to nothing: not love, not work. It is unforgivable of someone to leave a trace of his time on earth.

DADA, recognizing only instinct, condemns explanation a priori. According to it, we should exercise no control over ourselves whatsoever. We can no longer admit the dogma of morality and taste.

§II

We read the newspaper like any other mortal. Without meaning to depress anyone, it is fair to say that the word *DADA* lends itself fairly easily to puns. That's even part of the reason we have adopted it. We do not know how to treat any subject seriously, least of all ourselves. Therefore, everything written about DADA can only make us glad. There isn't a single human-interest anecdote for which we would not trade the entire history of art criticism. Anyway, the wartime press hardly prevented us from seeing Marshal Foch as a trickster and President Wilson as an idiot.

We ask nothing better than to be judged on appearances. The word has gone around that I wear glasses. If I told you why, you would never believe me. It's in memory of a grammar example: "Noses were made to hold up eyeglasses; therefore I wear eyeglasses." What's that you say? Oh, right: that really dates us.

Pierre is a man. But there is no DADA truth. One has only to utter a sentence for the opposite sentence to become DADA. I've seen Tristan Tzara asking mutely for a pack of cigarettes at the tobacconist's; I have no idea what was wrong with him. I can still hear Philippe Soupault insistently demanding live birds at the hardware store. As for myself, at this moment I might be dreaming.

All things considered, a red host is worth a white host. DADA does not claim to get you into Heaven. A priori it would be absurd to expect a DADA masterpiece in the fields of literature and painting. We no longer believe, of course, in the possibility of any social improvement, even if we despise conservatism above all and declare our support of any revolution, whatever it might stand for. "Peace at any price" was DADA's watchword in wartime, just as in peacetime DADA's watchword is "War at any price."

Contradiction is no more than an appearance, no doubt the most flattering of all. I speak and I have nothing to say. I do not claim the slightest ambition, although I might seem perfectly active to you: how could the idea that my right side is but the shadow of my left side, and vice versa, not leave me completely paralyzed? In the most general sense of the word, we pass for poets because above all we attack language, the worst convention there is. One can know the word *hello* and still say "farewell" to the woman one meets again after a year's separation.

In conclusion I wish to take only pragmatic objections into account. DADA uses your own reasoning against you. If we reduce you to claiming that it is more advantageous to believe, rather than not believe, in the teachings of all the religions of beauty, love, truth, and justice, it is only because you are not afraid to place yourselves at DADA's mercy, by agreeing to meet us on our chosen terrain, which is doubt.

The Cantos of Maldoror
by the Comte de Lautréamont [1]

Human life would not be such a disappointment for some of
us if we did not constantly feel empowered to accomplish acts
beyond our abilities. It seems that even miracles are within our
reach. We have made Christ into a man like any other so as to
stop harboring doubts about him. Certainly religions are not in
the least absurd: no belief could be more natural than that in
the immortality of the soul, or for that matter, in immortality,
period. (I have great trouble admitting that my heart will stop
beating someday.) At most we rise up against the idea of an ulti-
mate truth. It happens that certain minds—which are otherwise
generous—refuse to admire a finished cathedral. These individuals turn toward poetry, which fortunately has remained in the age
of persecutions. Religion, the common man believes, "never com-
mands one to do evil." On the other hand, what such individuals
can perceive of a poetic morality hardly inspires confidence that
poetry has much to recommend it.

It would nonetheless be a mistake to consider art an end in itself.
The doctrine of "art for art's sake" is just as reasonable as a doctrine of "life for art's sake" is, to my mind, insane. We now know
that poetry must lead somewhere. On this certainty rests, for example, our passionate interest in Rimbaud. But, as if to frustrate
our desire, the latter, like so many others when questioned about
the Beyond, has constantly disappointed us. One can see his letters from Abyssinia only as a series of jokes. The simplest way to

1. Concerning a new printing.

make a party lose interest is to remove both the player and the stakes simultaneously. History—literary or otherwise—does not flatter itself that it taught us what would have happened *if.* We would be guilty of a certain tactlessness if we honored someone simply because he died "in the flower of youth." Nor should we be influenced by a biography that is utterly devoid of anecdotes. The thing is that, to speak of Lautréamont, we must stick with his works. Isidore Ducasse has so completely vanished behind his pseudonym that today it would seem an exaggeration to identify this young tutor (?) with Maldoror, or even with the author of his *Cantos.*

The fact that such energies are being spent (provisionally, they believe) on writing is what warrants reflection. It is still in literary work, applied or otherwise, that one has the best chance of satisfying one's will to power. The *effect* one produces can be felt immediately, if we can take the word in its broadest sense. Only ink and paper can keep the imagination alert. They should not have made fun of that orator who got his ideas only as he was speaking. I believe that for the moderns, literature is becoming a powerful machine that is advantageously replacing the old ways of thinking. As a last resort, and counter to all loyalty, the best logicians try to win our agreement by means of an image. This is, said Lautréamont, because "metaphor does far more services to human aspirations toward the infinite than those imbued with prejudices as a rule try to represent." I understand that abuse of confidence is not serious and that it is in one's interest to encourage anything that can throw reason into doubt. The idea of contradictions, which remains current, seems nonsensical to me. From the unity of the body, we have been much too quick to believe in the unity of the soul; whereas we might harbor several consciousnesses, and their vote is quite capable of electing two contrary ideas in our internal ballot. This theory, in any case, perfectly concords with the little we now know about heredity.

The role of desire being to disappoint us, I'm glad that at this point it shows itself to be ineluctable. I won't even argue with the mysteries Lautréamont claims to reveal to me on page 243.[2] In chemistry two combined bodies can give off such heat, or generate such evident precipitation, that the experiment no longer interests me. Such preparations can still procure a veritable repose of the senses. It's strange that people blame poets for resorting to surprise, as if we were not always wishing for someone to fire a gun next to our ear so as to relieve us from paying attention for a few seconds.

This is also why we so enjoy laughing. For as long as the explosion lasts, its cause escapes us (this is a far cry from the mysticism of mystification of which we've heard tell). The pleasant "concern for dignity" common to all men, which Charlie Chaplin recently wrote about, can try all it likes to make us hold ourselves in check; such fits nonetheless deserve pride of place in the heart's geography. But Lautréamont does not escape the rule: laughter, "this shameful stripping away of human nobility," horrifies him. "Let's be serious," he repeats to himself. He would forever be caught out and would turn spiteful if his relativism did not come to his aid. It's just that, according to him, enthusiasm and internal coldness can indeed be *perfectly* allied, and he pushes human respect far enough to consider idleness and work equally sacred.

The time has not yet come to study the moral impact of Ducasse's opus. It can be deduced only through a comparison between *Maldoror* and the *Poésies;* the occasion seems better suited to speak of the latter. I cannot demand that the passage from one volume to the other pass for a revolution in time. I can only hope that readers of *Maldoror* will see beyond a pure Baudelaireanism of form. If not, they will live to regret it, all the more so in that Lautréamont's style would counter it with a stirring denial. "If death arrests the fantastic scrawniness of my shoulders' two long arms—employed in the lugubrious pounding of my literary gypsum—I want the mourning reader at least to be able to

2. This page in Breton's edition corresponds to p. 151 of *Maldoror and the Complete Works,* specifically the passage beginning "I do not think the reader will have ground for regret if he brings to my narrative . . ." (trans.)

say to himself: 'One must give him his due. He has considerably cretinized me.'" At bottom, no one will observe greater linguistic restraint. Lautréamont was so acutely aware of how unfaithful means of expression are that he never stopped treating them cavalierly: he forgave them nothing, and whenever necessary, he shamed them. Thus, in a certain way, he made their betrayal impossible. And therefore, since nothing can ever hope to be resolved by grammatical artifice, we should be grateful to him for suspending, as he does, the end of his sentence rather than pretending to solve—no matter how elegantly—a problem that will remain eternally posed.

For Dada

It is impossible for me to conceive of a mental joy other than as a breath of fresh air. How could it be comfortable within the limits in which nearly every book, every event, confines it? I doubt that even one person, at least once in his life, has not been tempted to deny the outside world. He would then realize that nothing is so serious or definite as all that. He would move on toward a revision of moral values, which would not prevent him from then returning to common law. Those who experienced this marvelous moment of lucidity at the cost of permanent disorientation are still called poets: Lautréamont, Rimbaud—but the fact is, literary childishness ended with them.

When will we grant arbitrariness the place it deserves in the creation of works or ideas? The things that touch us are generally less willed than we would believe. A felicitous expression or sensational discovery is announced in miserable fashion. Almost nothing achieves its goal, unless, exceptionally, something surpasses it. And the history of these gropings—psychological literature— is hardly instructive: despite its pretensions, no novel has ever proven anything. The most illustrious examples of the genre are not worth setting before our eyes; the most appropriate reponse we could give it is total indifference. Unable as we are to embrace at once the entirety of a painting, or a misfortune, where do we get the right to judge?

If young people have it in for convention, we should not dismiss them as ridiculous: who knows whether reflection makes good counsel? I intend to praise innocence wherever I find it, and I note that it is tolerated only in its passive form. This contradiction alone would be enough to make me skeptical. To keep oneself from being subversive means quelling everything that is not absolutely submissive. I see no valor in that. Revolts are plotted in solitude; there is no need to distance the storm from these ancient sacramental words.

Such considerations strike me as superfluous. I make statements for the pleasure of compromising myself. It should be against the law to use dubious modes of speech. The most convinced or authoritarian individual is not the one we think. I still hesitate to speak about what I know best.

SUNDAY[1]

The airplane weaves telegraph lines
and the source sings the same song
at the Coachman's Meeting House the drinks are orange
but the train mechanics have white eyes
The lady has lost her smile in the woods

The sentimentality of today's poets is something on which we should agree. From the concert of imprecations they so enjoy, a voice proclaiming that they have no soul occasionally rises to enchant them. One young man who at age twenty-three held the most beautiful gaze I know on the universe has mysteriously left us. It is easy for the critics to claim that he was bored: Jacques Vaché was not about to leave behind a last will and testament! I can still see him smiling as he pronounced the words *final wishes.* We are not pessimistic. The one who was painted lying on a reclining chair, so *fin-de-siècle* that he would not have been out of place among collections of psychological works, was the least weary and most subtle of us all. I still see him sometimes; in the trolley car a rider guides his provincial cousins down "Boulevard Saint-Michel: university quarter"; the trolley windows wink in connivance.

We have been chided for not confessing endlessly. Jacques Vaché's good fortune is never to have produced anything. He always kicked aside works of art, the ball-and-chain that retains

1. Philippe Soupault.

the soul after death. At the moment when, in Zurich, Tristan Tzara was launching his decisive proclamation—the Dada Manifesto of 1918—Jacques Vaché was unwittingly verifying its principal tenets. "A philosophical question: from which angle to start looking at life, god, ideas, or anything else. Everything we look at is false. I don't think the relative result is any more important than the choice of pastry or cherries for dessert."[2] A spiritual fact being given, there is some haste to see it reproduced in the moral sphere. "Make gestures," they call out to us. But, as André Gide will agree, "measured against the scale of Eternity, every action is vain,"[3] and we can make the effort required for a childish sacrifice. I am not merely situating myself in time. The scarlet waistcoat,[4] rather than the profound thinking of an era: that, unfortunately, is what everyone understands.

The obscurity of our words is constant. The riddle of meaning must remain in the hands of children. Reading a book to learn something denotes a certain simplicity. The little that the most famous works can teach us about their authors, or about their readers, should rapidly dissuade us from trying this experiment. It is the thesis that disappoints us, not its expression. I regret having to pass through these unclear sentences, receiving confidences without object, feeling at every moment, through the fault of some blabbermouth, a sense of knowing it already. The poets who have recognized this hopelessly flee the intelligible: they know that their work has nothing to lose. One can love an insane woman more than any other.

2. Tristan Tzara.

3. Although Breton might appear to be quoting Gide, this is a snippet (as was the preceding one) from Tzara's "Dada Manifesto 1918." The reference to "gestures" comes from a spectator's heckling at one of the first Dada demonstrations—as Gide had mockingly reported several months earlier in his own article on Dada (*La Nouvelle Revue Française,* 1 April 1920). (trans.)

4. A reference to poet Théophile Gautier's famous attire at the 1830 premiere of Victor Hugo's play *Hernani,* at which differences between Romantics and Classicists in the audience erupted into a full-scale brawl. In the current context the waistcoat symbolizes the purely scandalous side of Dada demonstrations rather than the deeper interrogation that some (notably Breton) sought to derive from them. (trans.)

> *Dawn fallen like a shower. The corners of the room are distant and solid. White plane. Comings and goings unmingled, in the shadows. Outside, in an alleyway with dirty children, with empty sacks that speak volumes, Paris by Paris, I discover. Money, the road, red-eyed journeys with luminous skulls. Daylight exists so that I can learn living, time. Ways-errors. Great agitate will become naked honey illness, poorly game already syrup, drowned head, weariness.*
>
> *Thought by happenstance, old flower of mourning, odorless, I hold you in my two hands. My head is shaped like a thought.*[5]

We are wrong to liken Dada to a subjectivism. No one who currently accepts the Dada label is aiming for hermiticism. "Nothing is incomprehensible," said Lautréamont. If I share the opinion of Paul Valéry—that "the human mind seems to me so made that it cannot be incoherent to itself"—I also think that it cannot be incoherent to anyone else. I believe that this requires not the extraordinary meeting of two individuals, or of one individual with the person he no longer is, but simply a series of acceptable misunderstandings, along with a small number of commonplaces.

Some have spoken of systematically exploring the unconscious. For poets, it is nothing new to let oneself go and write according to the vagaries of one's mind. The word *inspiration,* which for some reason has fallen into disuse, was once seen in a very favorable light. Almost every true imagistic innovation, for example, strikes me as being a spontaneous creation. Guillaume Apollinaire quite rightly thought that clichés such as "lips of coral," whose fortune could pass for a criterion of value, was the product of an activity that he termed *surrealist.* The origins of words themselves are probably no different. He went so far as to make of the principle that one should never build on a previous invention the very condition of scientific perfection and of "progress," so to speak. The idea of the human leg, lost in the wheel, resurfaced only by chance in the locomotive connecting rod. In the same way the biblical tone is starting to reemerge in poetry. I would be tempted to explain this latter phenomenon by the decreased

5. Paul Eluard.

intervention, or nonintervention, in the new writing processes, of personal choice.

What most effectively threatens to harm Dada in public opinion is the interpretation that two or three false sages have given of it. Up until now they have especially tried to see in it the application of a system that is enjoying a great vogue in psychiatry, Freud's "psychoanalysis"—an application, moreover, that the present author foresaw. Mr. H.-R. Lenormand even seems to believe that we would benefit from psychoanalytic treatment, if only one could make us submit to it. It goes without saying that the analogy between Cubist or Dadaist works and the ravings of the insane is highly superficial, but it is not yet proven that the so-called absence of logic absolves us from admitting a singular choice, that "plain" language has the disadvantage of being elliptical, and finally that only the works in question could show their authors' abilities and consequently give critics a reason for existing that they have always lacked:

> *At the school of infinite thoughts*
> *Of the most beautiful people*
> *Hymenoptera architectures*
> *The books I'd write would be madly tender*
> *If you were still*
> *In this novel composed*
> *At the top of the stairs*[6]

All this, moreover, is so relative that for every ten people who accuse us of being illogical, there is one who blames us for going to the opposite extreme. Mr. J.-H. Rosny, noting Tristan Tzara's declaration that "in the course of campaigns against every dogmatism and in a spirit of irony toward the creation of literary schools, Dada became the 'Dada movement,'" remarks, "Thus the origin of Dadaism is not the founding of a new school, but the repudiation of all schools. There is nothing absurd about such a viewpoint, quite the contrary: it is even logical, all too logical."

6. Francis Picabia.

No one has made any attempt to have Dada account for its will not to be considered a school. People love to insist on the words *group, ringleader,* and *discipline.* They even go so far as to claim that, in the guise of extolling individuality, Dada constitutes a real danger to it, without stopping to notice that we are especially bound together by our differences. Our shared exception to artistic or moral rules affords us only fleeting satisfaction. We are well aware that beyond this an inexpressible personal whim will have its way, which will be more "Dada" than the existing movement. This is what Jacques-Emile Blanche helped us to understand when he wrote: "Dada will survive only by ceasing to exist."

> *Let us draw the victim's name out of a hat*
> *Aggression hangman's noose*
>
> *The one who was speaking dies*
> *The murderer stands and says*
> *Suicide*
> *End of the world*
> *Furling of seashell flags.*[7]

To begin with, the Dadaists have taken pains to state that there is nothing they want. To know. No need to worry; the instinct for self-preservation always carries the day. When someone naively asked us—after a reading of the manifesto that goes, "No more painters, no more writers, no more religions, no more royalists, no more anarchists, no more socialists, no more police," and so on—whether we would "let humanity remain," we smiled, hardly wanting to put God on trial. Aren't we the last to forget that there are limits to understanding? If it so happens that I get such pleasure from these words by Georges Ribemont-Dessaignes, it's just that at bottom they constitute an act of extreme humility: "What is beautiful? What is ugly? What are big, strong, weak? What are Carpentier, Renan, Foch? Don't know. What is me? Don't know. Don't know, don't know, don't know."

7. Louis Aragon.

Gaspard de la Nuit
by Aloysius Bertrand[1]

After centuries of philosophy we are still living on the poetic
ideas of early man. When saying "Paradise" we point to the sky.
Abstract marvels respond to too specific a need to have any influence on our mores. In this regard Millet's *Angelus* provides a
better illustration than all the works of the great thinkers. The
role played in belief by the most banal aesthetic sense makes up
for a thousand pointless debates. An accidental death is translated
many years later in the country by a little cross erected on the
spot where the victim fell. It's all we wish to know. The word
revelation could be applied only to things that fit the meaning:
a word, a cure. In the presence of a supernatural phenomenon,
we never express anything other than delight or fear. The more
skeptical of us live in a haunted house. Biology, which these days
rejects spontaneous generation, accepts other principles that are
just as irrational. History chases its own tail. If "as the poet says"
is one of our common locutions, it is because through it we constantly attest to our haste to have done with the opposing party
by reaching the observatory from which one can see "an angel
descending, wings atremble, from the time of the stars."

Romanticism has laid itself open to a reaction that still obtains and that exposes a number of present and future works to
summary condemnation. We are absolutely determined to exter-
minate the Sioux Indians who, for men of another race, can be
distinguished only by their feathers. I believe that nothing is beneath criticism. They say that Turenne fainted at the sight of a
mouse. The power of that mouse, which is hardly negligible, does

1. Concerning a new printing.

not suffice to explain the genius of Turenne. As I see it, the same is true for Romantic moonlight and poison. Soon the sources of modern lyricism—machines, the daily newspaper—will in turn inspire no emotion. The failure of one of the most beautiful poetic discoveries of our time, hysteria, should warn us against an annoying tendency to generalize. We know today that there is no "hysterical mental state," and I am very near to thinking that there is no romantic mental state, either. Charcot had not counted on his patients' gift for simulation. Let's not forget that we all follow a fashion that changes every season.

Gaspard de la Nuit can be retained only as a milestone in literary history. In its way it makes us think that there exists no moral condition of beauty. With it we begin to take interest in something other than an obstacle course. It is inadmissible that language can insolently triumph over willed difficulties (prosody), that the poet's ambition is limited to being able to dance in the dark amid daggers and bottles. Baudelaire's wish—"Who is the man among us who has not dreamed of the miracle of a poetic prose, musical without rhythm or rhyme, supple and lively enough to adapt itself to the lyrical movements of the soul, the undulations of reverie, the shocks of perception?"—can very well be interpreted in this way. Of course, Aloysius Bertrand's prose falls far short of this ideal, and Baudelaire himself does not seem to have had any more luck with it. This is because both of them, when writing, never stopped putting themselves in the context of the "poem," so that a model of the genre was promptly established and one could learn the rules of this new game. From then on one could "compose" prose poems just like sonnets. Pierre Reverdy and Max Jacob have recently become masters of the form; it is unfortunate for them that the promissory notes have not retained their value. The charming distinction that the author of *The Dice Cup* tries to make between Rimbaud's poems and his own seems well-founded; still, I hope that he'll let me side with Rimbaud when the cut is made. My dear Max, the road to artistic hell is paved with intentions such as yours. On the other hand, the *Illuminations* have nothing to do with the metric system, and yet they were able to touch our most intimate selves; they could make us taste the delights of that "spiritual chase"[2] which for us is much more than a lost manuscript.

Our life is forever the House of the Ferryman. "In less time than it takes to write it," we are transported from one world to another. We mustn't confuse travel books with books that send us traveling. Despite everything, I'm glad that Bertrand takes pleasure in rushing us from the present into a past in which our assumptions immediately fall to shreds. I also praise him for resorting to dialogue whenever he wanted to foster misunderstanding. The text hasn't yet been written that would keep us from seeking the philosopher's stone. Humanity has not aged. In the night of Gaspard, what does it matter how long we have to stretch out our hands before we can feel one of these very fine rains that will soon yield an enchanted fountain?

2. "La Chasse spirituelle" was a lost (and perhaps an apocryphal) poem by Rimbaud, of which only the title had been preserved. The poem was briefly thought to have been discovered in 1949; the text that was alleged to be the poem was published to wide fanfare, but it soon proved to be a fake. Breton recounts the stages of the incident, as well as his own role in denouncing the forgery, in his essay "Flagrant délit" (in *La Clé des champs,* 1953). (trans.)

Max Ernst

The invention of photography dealt a mortal blow to old means of expression, as much in painting as in poetry, where automatic writing, which appeared toward the end of the nineteenth century, is a veritable photography of thought. Now that a blind instrument allowed them to reach with utter certainty the goal that they had hitherto set themselves, artists rashly claimed to be breaking with the imitation of appearances. Unfortunately human effort, which always varies the arrangement of existing elements, cannot be applied toward producing a single new element. A landscape in which nothing terrestrial figures is beyond the scope of our imagination. It is possible that, in denying such a landscape any affective value a priori, we refuse to conjure it. Moreover, it is equally sterile to constantly return to the standardized image of an object (a catalog illustration) or to the meaning of a word, as if it were up to us to rejuvenate them. We must pass beyond these meanings, so as then to distribute them, grouping them in whatever arrangements we please. Symbolism and Cubism failed from having been unaware of that essential freedom in its limitations.

It seems that the belief in an absolute space and time is disappearing. Dada does not claim to be modern. It also deems it pointless to subject oneself to the laws of a given perspective. Its nature keeps it from becoming attached even slightly to matter and from letting itself be intoxicated by words. But the marvelous ability to reach out, without leaving the field of our experience, to two distinct realities and bring them together to create a spark; to put within the grasp of our senses abstract figures with the same intensity, the same high relief as the others; and, by removing our systems of reference, to disorient us within our own memories—

that is what holds Dada's attention, for the time being. Doesn't such an ability make the person who possesses it better than a poet, since poets do not need to be aware of their visions and, in any case, maintain strictly platonic relations with them?

We still have to do away with a few rules, such as the rule of the three unities. Today, thanks to the cinema, we know how to make a locomotive *arrive* on canvas. As the use of acceleration and deceleration devices spreads, people should get used to seeing oak trees surge up and antelope soar. We eagerly look forward to seeing what this "relative time" we have heard about might be. Soon the expression "visible to the naked eye" will seem meaningless; in other words, we will perceive without a single blink of an eye the passage from birth to death, just as we'll become aware of infinitesimal variations. How easy it is to see this by applying this method to the study of a boxing match: the only mechanism that it threatens to paralyze in us is that of pain. Who knows whether, in this way, we are not preparing to someday escape the principle of identity?

Because, resolved to do away with still-life mystico-charlatanism, he projects before our eyes the most captivating film in the world, without losing the grace of smiling even as he illuminates the innermost depths of our internal life with an unparalleled light, we do not hesitate to see Max Ernst as the man of these infinite possibilities.

Ideas of a Painter

The seventh of November. Derain in his studio. No need to make small talk first. I admire a canvas depicting a wild boar hunt (for the apartment of the explorer Nansen). Derain turns out to be rather dissatisfied with it: the work lacks lyricism. One has to penetrate intimately the lives of the things one paints. Form for form's sake holds no interest. When I speak to someone, what do I know of this person's form? Nothing matters other than the pull of his senses toward me; only this gives me the impression of life. This in no way entails painting *Man* and not being able to paint *a man;* individual differences abide (one subject's external ear is all the larger for his being half deaf). Painting can claim no other resemblance. Form must tell us about function. Nothing to be sought beyond the senses. The same rule applies to animals and plants. The life of a tree is a mystery that no painter has ever managed to solve. Henri Rousseau, perhaps, was practically the only one to worry about this, and even then he could not see the forest for the leaves. At local fairs they sell a game that consists of trying to get a ring out of a wire labyrinth. It's the same problem as with the life of a tree (the winning painter is the one who can pull out the ring) or the life of an inanimate object. Who can claim to have grasped the "movement" of a fabric (immobility = absolute movement)? Everything that falls within the range of my senses plays a role for me; not to relate everything back to me would be either naive or hypocritical. Derain calls only physical life into question. The most captivating science is natural history. I stick a bean in the ground and ten more come up without my having used a single instrument: isn't that marvelous?

Take a ball. In painting it has never been considered anything more than a sphere; it has never been given anything more than a mathematical representation. And still, it is endowed with far more important properties: it rolls; placed on a flat surface, it wavers. It can also be elastic, and bounce. What have I said about the ball by making it round? The thing is to reproduce not an object but the *virtue* of that object, in the ancient sense of the word.

Simple as it may be, a view of that sort can topple the universe. Psychology and medicine will get something out of it. Biologists with their microscopes remind us of astrologists with their telescopes. Microorganisms, which are generally considered animals, are above all *figures of force,* just like astral emanations. The day will come when a physician can formulate his diagnostics simply by looking at the patient's face: there is certainly something about the lame man's face that limps. But too much wisdom threatens to compromise the world's peace: the ancients held these secrets, and perhaps they destroyed the library of Alexandria to counter a grave danger. Our entire struggle today is to rediscover these lost secrets.

Derain speaks with emotion about the *white dot* that certain Flemish or Dutch still-life painters of the seventeenth century used to highlight a vase or a fruit. Always mysteriously and admirably placed, this dot could not be perceived by them. It in fact bears no relation to the color of the object or its luminous sheen, and nothing justifies its presence in terms of composition. (We know that the artists in question frequented alchemists' laboratories.) This observation is crucial. If someone lights a candle in the dark and then draws it away from my eye until I can make out only the flame, the height of that flame and my distance from it elude me. It becomes no more than a white dot. The object I paint or the creature before me does not live until I have made this white dot appear on it. The important thing is to place the candle well.

Why, in such conditions, shouldn't one *sign* the black cardboard frame that stands out on the whitewashed wall? The painter is led to study his model through a series of similar rectangular frames of different sizes and colors. (The first thing the owner of these paintings did was to have them framed.) Without this artifice, how could one paint the sky that stretches everywhere above him? The case of Matisse is instructive: he now paints himself behind his canvases, placing himself in his thoughts behind himself. For all that, Derain is not tempted to sign the black frame. It is important to *prove,* demonstrate, which the frame does not do. If I present it as something other than the image of what I'm striving toward, perfection and death, it becomes a satanic figure. Let's not forget that we are obliged to pass via matter. The latter is valuable particularly because it makes us despair and because only despair is not sterile. (We choose art only as a means of despairing.) This is what Renoir understood better than Cézanne: he holds up against any test we subject him to. Derain makes Corot out to be one of the greatest geniuses of the Western world. We are nowhere near exhausting the mysteries of his art. Cézanne, on the other hand, is hanging on by a mere thread. His painting is flattering like rice powder. This man, who has captured the world's attention, was perhaps completely mistaken.

Everything that the Egyptians, the Greeks, and the Renaissance Italians did *is.* A host of modern works are not. We do not pay enough attention to the era in which we live. To those who would observe that these are not the ideas of a painter, we can answer that it is impossible to have any other ideas today. Can one still claim to find a "natural" man?

Derain is not a subjectivist. He denies that a collection of indifferent strokes can appear beautiful. The three curves I see here affect me only because they form the astrological sign for Leo. Nothing more premeditated than that. We could say as much about the letters of the alphabet. The appearance of a page of characters in a book is extremely unnerving: to think that *that* can make people act. Derain admits that language (pictorial or otherwise) is a convention, but he believes he can go beyond this. Asked to comment on Picabia's project (assemble some twenty balls in the corner of a pool table, then sweep them forward in a single motion along the felt, photograph the result, and sign it), he demurs. That would be a feat of magic rather than a work of art. In any case, to reach some sort of conclusion one would have to take *several* photos of the pool table once the balls were in place, in order to compare them.

Derain willingly admits that provocation is excluded from his most recent works. Moreover, that's how he wants it. His earlier "distortions" most often had their reason for being in the *rhythm* that a painter is forced to observe. (A head removed from the torso might be round, but placed on shoulders it stretches out. With only the contours of the head, the painter must make eyes and a mouth appear without drawing them.) But Derain also believed that *lyricism* demanded that the bowl should be larger than the armoire, that a factory building should occupy the entire landscape. Now he believes that he should grant each object its conventional space. The truly lyrical man is one who lies.[1]

1. May André Derain forgive the unauthorized publicity given to his spontaneous statements, which I do not claim to endow with any definitive character—an hour of unrehearsed conversation never yet having committed anyone to anything.

Giorgio de Chirico

"When Galileo rolled two balls down an inclined plane after having determined their weight, or when Torricelli made the air carry a weight that he knew to be equal to a certain column of water, then a new light shone on all of physics."

We have an imperfect idea of the seven wonders of the ancient world. In our day, a few sages—Lautréamont, Apollinaire—have destined the umbrella, the sewing machine, and the top hat for universal admiration. With the certainty that nothing is incomprehensible and that everything, if need be, can serve as a symbol, we are spending the treasures of imagination. Once it was poetic to depict the Sphinx as a lion with a woman's head. I believe that a veritable modern mythology is being formed. It falls to Giorgio de Chirico to fix it indelibly in our memory.

God made man in his image, and man made the statue and the mannequin. The need to consolidate the first (pedestal, tree trunk), the second's adaptation to its function (piece of varnished wood replacing head and arms)—these occupy all the painter's thoughts. There is no doubt that the style of our dwellings interests him in the same way, as do the tools already built by us in view of new constructions: square, protractor, geographical map.

The nature of his mind especially predisposed him to revising the perceptible data of time and space. The branches of the family tree are flowering all over the place. A certain orange light appears simultaneously as a candle flame and a starfish. Dihedral angles. At the same time, Chirico does not think that a ghost can enter other than through a door.

None of this would seem to have anything to do with painting.

But we know the Colossus of Rhodes and the Temple of Ephesus thanks to Philo of Byzantium, a Greek engineer and tactician, author of treatises on the art of laying siege and the manufacture of war machines (end of the third century B.C.).

André Gide Speaks to Us
of His Selected Works

I have never been a familiar of André Gide's, which no doubt allows me to meet him from time to time and to engage in conversation that is a little less vapid than he would like. To tell the truth, although frivolity is not my strong point, the author of *Lafcadio's Adventures* (these periphrases suit him) amuses me, and has for a long time now, much more than he worries me. The further along I go, the more affection I'll have for a man who is mistaken. In our day and age there is a ready-made criterion: his superficiality, his flirtatiousness, his pretensions, balanced out by some second-rate finer qualities, tell me as much about those who admire him as about those he exasperates.

The scene takes place, one of these past few days, at tea time, in a pastry shop on Rue de Grenelle.

GIDE: Really, what do you want from me? Didn't my anthology, which just came out with the NRF, give you complete satisfaction?

I: I'm sorry, Monsieur, I haven't read it.

GIDE: Here's a copy. But don't ask me to sign it. It would give me great pleasure, but I haven't done it for anyone.

I: If I'm not mistaken, you published a similar work in the "Adolescents' Library."

GIDE: If only you knew what a game I'm forced to play. Just because I'm not a poet! Poets have all the luck. But I can't tell you how hard *I* have to think before moving a single one of my pawns! I still have a lot to write, but I know my goals, and I've even drawn up the plan of all my works. You can be sure that I'm moving ahead—slowly, I admit, but all the more pleasurably.

1: Aren't you afraid that people will give you scant credit for all this planning? It has to do with something else entirely. By trying not to miss any opportunities, you might still lose the game.

GIDE: I won't owe any explanations until after my death. And what difference does it make, since I'm quite certain *I'll* be the one wielding the greatest influence fifty years from now!

1: So why are you so concerned with keeping up appearances? We know what legend you'd like people to build up around you: your anxiety, your horror of dogma, your deceptive side. Even the worst hacks are trying their hands at it.

GIDE: On the contrary, I'm more prone to slander than ever before. Henri Massis has just heaped abuse on me in the *Revue universelle*. Believe me, Breton, everything will have its day: by reading my selected works, you'll see I was especially thinking of you and your friends.

1: A preference isn't enough for us. There's not a single one of us who wouldn't trade all your books to see you pin down that little gleam you made flash once or twice, I mean in the glances of Lafcadio and "A German."[1] Is it really worth spending time on anything else?

GIDE: What you're saying is very strange, but your feeling seems to concern the failure of humanity as a whole. I understand you better than you think, and I feel sorry for you. As Paul Valéry and I were saying the other day, "What can a man do?" And he added, "Do you remember Cervantes's admirable question: 'How can you conceal a man?' "

1. A reference to Gide's "Conversation avec un Allemand quelques années avant la guerre" (*Nouvelle Revue Français,* 1 August 1919), in which his young German interlocutor notably remarks that writing is, for him, strictly a financial necessity and that "the work of art is only a last resort": "Action is what I want; yes, the most intense action . . . intense . . . to the point of murder." (trans.)

Interview with Doctor Freud

To the young people and romantic souls who, because psycho-analysis happens to be in vogue this winter, need to imagine one of the most prosperous branch offices of modern charlatan-ism (Doctor Freud's consulting room) as being fitted out with machines for turning rabbits into hats and soft determinism for a desk blotter, I am not displeased to say that the greatest psy-chologist of the age lives in an unassuming house tucked away in an obscure Vienna neighborhood. "Dear Sir," he had written me, "having very little time in these days, I would ask you to come see me on Monday (tomorrow, the 10th) at 3 P.M. in my office. Yours very truly, Freud."

A modest plaque at the entrance: "Dr. Freud, 2–4"; a not very attractive servant girl; a waiting room whose walls are decorated with four mildly allegorical engravings—Water, Fire, Earth, and Air—and with a photograph depicting the master among his col-laborators; a dozen or so patients of the most pedestrian sort; and once, after the sound of a bell, several shouts in succession—not enough here to fill even the slimmest of reports. This until the famous padded door cracks open for me. I find myself in the presence of a little old man with no style who receives clients in a shabby office worthy of the neighborhood G P. Ah! he doesn't much like France, the only country to have remained indifferent to his work. Still, he proudly shows me a pamphlet that has just been published in Geneva, which is nothing more than the first French translation of five of his lessons. I try to make him talk by throwing names such as Charcot and Babinski into the con-versation, but either because the memories I'm calling on are too dim or because he maintains a posture of cautious reticence with strangers, I can get him to speak only in generalities, such as "Your letter, the most moving I've ever received," or "Fortunately, we have great faith in the young."

The New Spirit

On Monday, 16 January, at 5:10 P.M., Louis Aragon was walking up Rue Bonaparte when he saw coming toward him a young woman in a tan-and-brown plaid tailored suit, wearing a cap made from the same fabric as her dress. She seemed to be very cold, despite the relatively mild temperature. Thanks to the light coming from the bookstore Le Coq, Aragon noted that she was of uncommon beauty and in particular that her eyes were huge. He wanted to go talk to her but remembered that he was carrying only two francs and twenty centimes. He was still thinking about her when André Breton joined him at the Deux Magots café. "I've just had an extraordinary encounter," said the latter the moment he sat down. "Walking up Rue Bonaparte, I passed a young woman who kept glancing over her shoulder, even though she seemed not to be waiting for anyone. A little before Rue Jacob she pretended to be absorbed in the display window of the prints shop, until an unbelievable, utterly vile passerby who had noticed her engaged her in conversation. They took a few steps together and stopped to talk, while I stood watching some distance away. Soon they parted, and the woman seemed to be even more disoriented. She retraced her steps for a moment; then, spotting a rather mediocre-looking character crossing the street, she suddenly went up to him. A few seconds later they dove into the Clichy-Odéon bus. I wasn't able to catch up to them. I noticed that they stayed on the rear platform, while a bit farther up the street the fat man from before was standing still, as if filled with remorse."

Aragon, as we said, seemed especially to have been struck by the stranger's beauty; Breton, by her very proper attire, her "young girl just getting out of school" aspect, with something extraordinarily *lost* in her bearing. Was she on drugs? Had she just suffered a tragedy? Aragon and Breton had great difficulty understanding the passionate interest they both took in this missed adventure. The latter was certain that, although he had seen the woman leave on the bus, she was still at the same place on Rue Bonaparte. He wanted to be sure. Walking out of the café he met André Derain, who promised to join him there in a few minutes.

"I've come back empty-handed," Breton told Aragon soon afterward. Neither one could get over his disappointment and, when Derain showed up, they couldn't help telling him the reason for their upset. They had no sooner begun than Derain cut them off: "A plaid suit," he cried. "But I just saw her near the fence at Saint-Germain-des-Prés. She was with a black man. He was laughing, and I even heard him say, 'Something will have to change.' Before that I'd seen this woman from a distance stopping other people, and for a moment I'd even expected her to come talk to me. I'm sure I've never seen her around here before, though I know every hooker in the neighborhood."

At six o'clock Louis Aragon and André Breton, unable to give up the idea of finding the key to the riddle, searched through part of the sixth arrondissement—but in vain.

After Dada

My friends Philippe Soupault and Paul Eluard will not contradict me if I say that "Dada" was never seen by us as anything more than the vulgar image of a state of mind that it in no way helped to create. If it occurs to them, as it did to me, to reject the label and realize the abuse to which they have fallen victim, perhaps this first principle will be saved. In the meantime they will forgive me for informing the readers of *Comoedia,* in order to remove all misunderstanding, that Mr. Tzara had no part in the invention of the word *Dada*—as attested by a letter from Schad and Huelsenbeck, his companions in Zurich during the war, which I am quite prepared to publish—and that he no doubt had very little hand in writing the "Dada Manifesto 1918," which determined our welcome and the credit we extended him.

The paternity of the manifesto is, in any case, formally claimed by Val Serner, a doctor of philosophy who lives in Geneva and whose German-language manifestoes, written before 1918, have not been translated into French. We know, furthermore, that the conclusions reached by Francis Picabia and Marcel Duchamp even before the war, alongside those reached by Jacques Vaché in 1917, would have been sufficient to orient us in and of themselves. Up until now I had been reluctant to denounce Mr. Tzara's bad faith and had let him blatantly arm himself with the proxy votes of the very individuals whose pockets he had picked in their absence. But today, when he is trying to grab his last chance to make some noise by falsely declaring his opposition to one of the most impartial enterprises that could be,[1] I have no qualms about ordering him to be silent.

1. The Congress of Paris (for the determination and defense of the modern spirit), April 1922.

Dada, thank goodness, is no longer an issue, and its funeral in around May 1921 engendered no brawls. The procession, numbering very few people, followed in the wake of Cubism-Futurism, which the students at the Beaux-Arts went to drown in effigy in the Seine. Although it had, as they say, its hour of fame, Dada left few regrets: in the long run its omnipotence and tyranny had made it unbearable.

Nonetheless I noted with some bitterness at the time that several of those who had given it handouts—generally those who had given the smallest handouts—found themselves reduced to poverty. The others lost no time in rallying around Francis Picabia's strong statements, inspired, as we know, only by a love of life and a horror of all corruption. Which is not to say that Picabia meant to re-create our unity around himself—

It's hard to imagine
How stupid and stolid success can make people[2]

—and he is more prepared than anyone to do without it. But, although there is no question of substituting a new group for our individual tendencies (Mr. Tzara must be joking), Louis Aragon, Pierre de Massot, Jacques Rigaut, Roger Vitrac, and I could not long remain indifferent to the marvelous detachment from all things of which Picabia gave us the example and that we are happy to state here.

For myself, I point out that this attitude is not new. If I abstained last year from taking part in the demonstrations organized by *Dada* at the Galerie Montaigne, it was because this sort of activity had already lost its attraction for me—because I saw in it the means of reaching my twenty-sixth or thirtieth birthday without striking a single blow, and I am determined to flee anything that masks itself in that kind of facility. In an unpublished article of the time, which few people have read, I deplored the stereotyped character that our gestures were taking on, and I wrote, verbatim,

2. The statement, seemingly by Picabia, is actually an excerpt from Apollinaire's "Victory" (in *Calligrammes*). (trans.)

"After all, the issue is not our insouciance or momentary good humor. Personally, I have no wish to be amused. It seems to me that sanctioning a series of utterly futile 'Dada' acts means seriously compromising one of the attempts at liberation to which I remain the most strongly attached. These ideas, which count among the finest, are at the mercy of their too-rapid popularization.

"Our age might well be ill-disposed toward concentration, but must we always accept being content with superficialities? 'The mind,' it has been said, 'is not so independent that it cannot be distracted by the slightest disturbance made around it.' What, then, can we predict for it if it insists on making that disturbance itself?"

Still today, it is hardly my intention to act as a judge. "The place and the formula"[3] might always elude me, but—and this cannot be said often enough—the important thing is this quest and nothing else. Hence the great void that we are forced to create in ourselves. Without going so far as to develop a taste for the pathetic, I am prepared to do without practically everything. I do not wish to slip on the waxed floor of sentimentality. There is no error, properly speaking: at most one could call it an unlucky wager, and those who are reading me are free to feel that the game is not worth the candle. For myself, I will try once more to involve myself even further, if possible—without, however, making Francis Picabia's words ("One must be a nomad, cross through ideas as one crosses through countries or cities") into a rule of hygiene or a duty. Even if every idea were fated to disappoint us, I would still take it as my starting point to devote my life to them.

3. This expression, cited by Breton on numerous occasions, is from Rimbaud's poem "Vagabonds." (trans.)

Leave Everything

For two months now I've been living in Place Blanche. Winters there are among the mildest, and on the sidewalk of this café devoted to the sale of intoxicants, women make brief and charming appearances. Nights exist hardly more than in the hyperborean realms of legend. I don't remember having lived anywhere else; those who say they knew me must be mistaken. But no, they even add that they thought I had died. You're right to call me to order. After all, who is speaking here? André Breton, a man of no special courage who until now has contented himself as best he could with some insignificant actions, and this because one day he might have felt too rigidly and definitively incapable of doing what he wanted. And it's true; I know I have already undone myself several times over. It's true that I find myself less than a monk, less than an adventurer. Still, I do not despair of getting back on my feet, and at the dawn of 1922, in lovely, festive Montmartre, I'm dreaming of what I might still become.

These days we make an idea out of the precipitation of everything into its opposite and the solution of both into a single category, which is itself reconcilable with the initial term, and so on until the mind attains the absolute idea, the reconciliation of every opposition and the unity of every category. If "Dada" had been that, of course it would not have been so bad, although to Hegel's sleep on his laurels I prefer the lively existence of the first little streetwalker to come along. But Dada is quite removed from such considerations. The proof is evident today, when its great trick is to pass itself off as a vicious circle ("Someday you will know that before Dada, after Dada, without Dada, for Dada, against Dada, despite Dada, is still Dada") without noticing that by that very token it is depriving itself of any virtue or effectiveness. Dada is amazed to see that it now has only a few poor devils on its side, who, huddled up in their poetry, emote like good bourgeois over the memory of its already ancient misdeeds. The danger long ago moved elsewhere. And what does it matter if, going his sorry little way, Mr. Tzara must one day share his glory with Marinetti or Baju! It has been said that I change men the way most people change socks. Kindly allow me this luxury, as I can't keep wearing the same pair forever: when one stops fitting, I hand it down to my servants.

I love and deeply admire Francis Picabia, and you can rehash several of the quips he has made at my expense without offending me. Every attempt has been made to mislead him about my true feelings, since it is clear that an understanding between us would make a few "sedentaries" feel much less secure. Dadaism, like so many other things, was for certain people no more than a means of sitting down. What I did not say in the preceding remarks is that there can be no absolute idea. We are subject to a kind of mental mimicry that forbids us from delving deeply into anything and makes us look harshly on what was once so dear. To give one's life for an idea, whether Dada or the one I am developing right now, could show proof only of great intellectual indigence. Ideas are neither good nor evil; they simply are. All the same to me whether they please or displease; they are much more worthy when they impassion me in one direction or another. Pardon me for thinking that, unlike ivy, I die when I become attached. Should I worry that my words might damage the cult of friendship that, according to Mr. Binet-Valmer's powerful remark, leads straight to the cult of patriotism?

I can only assure you that I don't give a damn about any of this and repeat:

Leave everything.
Leave Dada.
Leave your wife, leave your mistress.
Leave your hopes and fears.

Drop your kids in the middle of nowhere.

Leave the substance for the shadow.

Leave behind, if need be, your comfortable life and promising
   future.

Take to the highways.

Clearly

A romantic current, born of the *poetic* agitation of these past years, had put several individuals at odds who up until then had expressed a common desire, both here[1] and elsewhere. At the height of the crisis (August 1921–March 1922) and on the eve of its resolution (July–August 1922), *Littérature* ceased publication. In the meantime Philippe Soupault and I tried without great success to create a diversion: the "top hat" issues.[2] But we soon realized that we were living on a compromise.

Today a certain obscurity surrounds this episode in the history of *Littérature,* in which Dada took possession, so to speak, of a little yellow-covered magazine that at the outset had enjoyed such a distinguished reputation. It is an unfortunate fact that Tristan Tzara's arrival in Paris appears to be not unrelated to this modification—although as I see it, that was infinitely less relevant than, for instance, my meeting in 1915 with Jacques Vaché, and especially the news of the latter's death, which I received like a blow

1. In *Littérature.*

2. Founded in March 1919, *Littérature* had initially had a much more traditional form and content, leading Breton later to dismiss the magazine as "well bred." This first incarnation lasted for twenty issues and had a plain yellow cover. After the August 1921 number, covering Dada's "trial" of novelist Maurice Barrès, the magazine ceased publication for several months; it reappeared in a "new series" in March 1922 with a cover featuring a top hat by Man Ray. By September this format, too, had been abandoned, in favor of a somewhat more adventurous magazine whose covers bore aggressive visual puns by Picabia. *Littérature* folded in June 1924 to make way for *La Révolution surréaliste.* (trans.)

to the heart around February 1919.[3] Nonetheless I admit having projected onto Tzara some of the hopes that Vaché, if lyricism had not been his element, would never have disappointed. This is also, no doubt, why someone like Huelsenbeck was taken in— Huelsenbeck, who, moreover (in a text reproduced *in extenso* in the present issue), levels charges against Tzara that seem to me entirely justified.

Literature, which some of my friends and I use with well-known disdain, is not something we treat as an illness (we were forced to employ these vulgar images). I would write, I would do nothing else, if to the question "Why do you write?" I could answer in all certainty, "I write because it's *still* what I do best." This is not the case, and I also think that poetry, which is all I have ever appreciated in literature, emanates more from the lives of human beings—whether writers or not—than from what they have written or from what we might imagine they could write. We must be wary of a large misunderstanding here: life, as I see it, is not the sum total of actions that can ultimately be ascribed to an individual (regardless of whether they are determined by the scaffold or the dictionary) but rather the way in which he seems to have accepted the unacceptable human condition. It goes no further than that. I'm not sure why, but it is still in the domains bordering literature and art that life, thus conceived, tends to reach its veritable fulfillment.

Like it or not, there are people who more or less shared that anxiety. Their great concern today is to let none of that show: to hear them tell it, they have always practiced art as a trade. Several days ago, at the home of a photographer friend of mine, I met Mr. Henri-Matisse (hyphenated). No artist wishes to be seen as having his way with nature any less easily. His earlier works? Mere sketches, whose only merit in his eyes is that they allowed him to reach his current *achievements*. There are a dozen like him today: the Valérys, Derains, and Marinettis, tumbling into the

3. Breton actually met Vaché in early 1916 and received news of his death in January 1919. In giving these slightly inaccurate dates, he (unconsciously?) extended his relationship with his late friend by at least several months. (trans.)

ditch one by one, who jokingly receive your condolences and take their leave after having sententiously made a date with you for ten years hence.

There are others, such as Mr. Cocteau, whose name I would apologize for dragging in here if I did not think it urgent to mention that they are living on their predecessors' corpses and if their ravings did not end up causing us an intolerable malaise. Whoever has not read Mr. Cocteau's letter in *L'Intransigeant,* in which he undertakes to reveal his "ars poetica," cannot know what an author with a gift both for sheer wrongheadedness and for de-idealization can wreak in such a delicate sphere.

Thank God, our age is less degraded than people say: Picabia, Duchamp, and Picasso are still with us. I am happy to see you, Louis Aragon, Paul Eluard, Philippe Soupault, my dear life-long friends. Do you remember Guillaume Apollinaire and Pierre Reverdy? Isn't it true that we owe a little of our strength to them? But already Jacques Baron, Robert Desnos, Max Morise, Roger Vitrac, and Pierre de Massot are waiting for us. Never let it be said that Dadaism served any purpose other than to keep us in a state of perfect readiness, from which we now head clear-mindedly toward that which beckons us.

Reply to a Survey [1]

Written poetry is losing its reason to exist with each passing day. If works such as those by Ducasse, Rimbaud, or Nouveau enjoy such prestige among the young, for starters it is because none of these authors made writing their profession (wasn't it one of them who had the last word on the subject: "A writers's hand is no better than a ploughman's. I will never have my hand"?).[2] It's just that their attitudes as human beings leave their merits as writers far behind, and that only these attitudes give true meaning to the works we admire. These works take on the character of a manifesto, in which we try to detect first and foremost the premeditation of the writers' attitudes. If we could make these attitudes count above all else, contemporary values would crumble.

Without feeling the same assurance about their authors (no one can predict the future), I would say that every current work that is even slightly remarkable, from Valéry to Picabia via Reverdy and Drieu la Rochelle, gives us at least a minimum of satisfaction in this regard. The rest, everything that people generally discuss, is of no importance. Personally I am incapable of taking talent into account. Poetry would hold no interest for me whatsoever if I didn't expect it to suggest to me and some of my friends a specific solution to the problem of our lives.

This said, do not expect me to enumerate the poetic schools

1. "What principal movements do you see in the younger generation of French poets, and what direction do you think poetry will take in the future?" (*Le Figaro*).

2. From Rimbaud, *A Season in Hell*. As with the line from "Vagabonds" quoted previously in "After Dada," this pronouncement—one of Breton's rallying cries—would become a favorite reference. (trans.)

currently in operation. I know nothing of Fantasism or Dada. The only real groups, as I see it, are, to be sure:

1. all artisans of the pen without distinction;

2. younger poets who, after having pretended (no doubt for opportunistic reasons) to understand what it was all about, are now falling under the preceding category (we could cite, to varying degrees, André Gide, Max Jacob, Paul Morand, etc.); and

3. those whose destinies have not yet filled me with despair: three or four individuals, myself included. Moreover, nothing proves that we hold the key to tomorrow's poetry. For that, obviously, one might as well read *Parisette*[3] and the cross-examinations of court trials.

3. An enormously popular serial novel, based on an equally popular film, about the adventures of a pretty young chorus dancer. The last installment appeared while Breton was drafting this "Reply." (trans.)

Marcel Duchamp

It is around this name, a veritable oasis for those who are still *searching,* that a particularly devastating assault might be waged, one capable of freeing modern consciousness from that terrible mania for fixation that we have always denounced. The famous intellectual manchineel tree[1] that in the space of half a century bore the fruits called Symbolism, Impressionism, Cubism, Futurism, and Dadaism needs only to be felled. The case of Marcel Duchamp today offers us a precious boundary line between two spirits that are finding themselves in increasing opposition within the very heart of the "modern spirit," depending on whether or not the latter claims to possess the truth, which is rightly depicted as an ideal nude who emerges from the well only to turn around and drown herself in the mirror.

A face whose admirable beauty cannot be attributed to any particularly affecting feature, just as anything one might say to the man dulls against a slab so polished that it reveals none of what is going on deep down; a twinkling eye to go with it, without sarcasm or self-indulgence, which dispels the slightest shadow of concentration and evinces a concern for remaining, externally, utterly amiable; elegance at its most fatal, and beyond elegance a truly supreme *ease*—that is how Marcel Duchamp appeared to me on his last visit to Paris: Duchamp, whom I had never seen and whose intelligence, thanks to the few details I'd picked up, struck me as marvelous.

And first of all, let us note that Marcel Duchamp's situation with respect to the contemporary movement is unique in that

---

1. The expression comes from Ducasse's *Poésies.* The manchineel, found in tropical America, has poisonous fruit and a milky sap that causes severe skin blisters. According to legend, even its shade is deadly. (trans.)

the most recent groups more or less take his name as an autho-
rization, without our being able to say how much he ever sanc-
tioned this, and whereas we see him detach himself from these
groups with complete freedom, even before a particular cluster
of ideas—whose originality largely derives from him—has taken
on that systematic cast that eliminates others. Could it be that
Marcel Duchamp reaches the *critical point* of ideas faster than anyone else? In any case, if one considers the evolution of his output,
it seems that his early adherence to Cubism was tempered by a
kind of advance nod to Futurism (1912: *The King and Queen Sur-
rounded by Swift Nudes*) and that his contribution to both did not
exclude, very early on, reservations of a Dadaistic nature (1915:
The Chocolate Grinder). Dada itself will have no greater luck in
overcoming his doubts: the proof is that in 1920, when there
was nothing more to be expected from it and when Tzara, who
was organizing the Dada Salon, felt authorized to include Marcel
Duchamp among the exhibitors, the latter cabled from America
the simple words "Nuts to you" [*pode bal*], which obliged Tzara
to replace the anticipated paintings with enlargements of the relevant catalog numbers and allowed him only poorly to save face.[2]

Let there be no mistake: we haven't the slightest intention
of codifying the modern spirit nor, for the simple enjoyment of
mysteries, of turning our backs on those who make a show of re-
solving them. Let the day come when, her riddle answered, the
Sphinx throws herself into the sea. But up until now there have
been only simulations. We have gathered and we shall continue
to gather in the hope of witnessing a conclusive experience. Let
us be, if you will, as ridiculous and touching as spiritualists, but
let us beware, my friends, of any sort of materialization. Cubism
is a materialization in corrugated cardboard, Futurism in rubber,
Dadaism in blotter paper. Moreover, I ask you, could anything
do us more harm than a *materialization*?

2. By the time the "Dada Salon" opened at the Galerie Montaigne in June
1921 (not 1920, as the text has it), Breton's rift with Dada was such that he did
not even attend. He was evidently gratified by Duchamp's similar nonpartici-
pation, for he recounted this anecdote in several of his works. (trans.)

Whatever you say, the belief in immateriality is not a materialization. Let us leave some of our friends grappling with these grotesque tautologies and return to Marcel Duchamp, who is the opposite of a doubting Thomas. I've seen Duchamp do an extraordinary thing: toss a coin in the air while saying, "Tails I leave for America tonight, heads I stay in Paris." *No* indifference involved; in all probability he would infinitely have preferred to leave, or to stay. But isn't personal choice—whose independence Duchamp is one of the first to have proclaimed by signing, for instance, a factory-made object—the most tyrannical of all, and isn't it right to put it to such a test, as long as one does not replace it with a mysticism of chance?

Ah! if only that coin could take a month to land, or a year; how clearly everyone would hear us then! Fortunately things are decided in the space of a breath—naturally it has to be carried out—and one had better have sufficient lung capacity to start all over again immediately. (It goes without saying that understanding the preceding remarks will remain the privilege of a few who can also appreciate—for their greater entertainment, alas!—this sentence written by a man who, at bottom, remained a stranger to such speculations, Guillaume Apollinaire; a sentence that gives the just measure of that prophetic capacity he so prized: "It will perhaps be reserved for an artist as uninvolved in aesthetic preoccupations, as concerned with energy as Marcel Duchamp, to reconcile Art and the People.")

In writing these lines, despite the extremely ambitious title under which I've gathered them, I hardly thought to exhaust the subject of Marcel Duchamp. My only wish was to avoid the same errors made by Apollinaire or Dada in his regard, and still more to ruin any future systematization of Duchamp's *attitude,* as it cannot help appearing to simple minds with their "love of novelty." I know, Duchamp does little more than play chess these days, and he would be satisfied with someday proving to be unbeatable at it. One might say that this is the stand he has taken on intellectual equivocation: if you wish, he will agree to pass for an artist, and even for a man who produced little because *he couldn't do otherwise.*

And so he, who has delivered us from the concept of blackmail-lyricism with its clichés (about which I'll have more to say later), returns to being a symbol for most people. I refuse to see this as anything other than a booby trap on his part. Personally, as I said, what I consider to be Marcel Duchamp's strength, what allowed him to walk away intact from several guillotines, is above all his *disdain of messages,* which will always confound those less favored.

Regarding what is to come, I think it would be wise for us to focus our attention on this disdain, and to do that we need only to think of the glass painting to which Duchamp will soon have devoted ten years of his life, which is not the "unknown master-piece" and around which, even before its completion, the most fabulous legends are being woven. Or else we should recall one of those odd spoonerisms whose author signs as Rrose Sélavy and that deserve special examination:

> *Conseil d'hygiène intime:*
> *Il faut mettre la moelle de l'épée dans le poil de l'aimée.*

> *[Personal hygiene tip:*
> *You must put the marrow of the sword into the pubis of the be-loved.]*[3]

For Marcel Duchamp, the question of art and life, or any other question that is liable to divide us at present, does not even arise.

---

3. A looser rendering of this spoonerism, by Elmer Peterson, goes, "Should you put the hilt of the foil in the quilt of the goil?" See his translation of Marcel Duchamp, *Salt Seller* (New York: Oxford University Press, 1973). (trans.)

The Mediums Enter

An unforeseen maneuver, a little nothing that—eyes half-closed on each other—we did not dare predict might make us put aside our quarrels, has just set back in motion the famous steam-swing near which, once upon a time, we would meet even without arrangement. It has been almost two years since the strange see-saw stopped working, after having scattered us rather forcefully in all directions; since then we've been trying with varying degrees of grace to remake its acquaintance. I have already had occasion to say that if we hurled responsibility for the breakdown back and forth at each other, no doubt without rhyme or reason, at least there was not a single one of us who regretted having taken a seat in that compartment ill-lit by the knees of young women, the compartment that beats time between houses.

No doubt about it, here we are again: Crevel, Desnos, and Péret on one side, Eluard, Ernst, Morise, Picabia, and myself on the other. We'll soon see how our positions differ. Right now, and with no second thoughts, I will add that there are three men whose presence at our side strikes me as indispensable, three men whom I have seen act in the most affecting way possible during a previous *departure* and who, owing to a deplorable circumstance (their absence from Paris), know nothing as yet about these preparations: Aragon, Soupault, and Tzara. May they allow me to make them virtual associates in our quest, along with all those who have not despaired of us, who remember having shared our initial conviction and, in spite of ourselves, never thought it could fall prey to its misadventures.

The unusual angle under which I relate the following facts would justify many, many precautions. Certainly the word *litera-*

ture, which can be found yet again on the masthead of these pages, has long seemed to be a purely whimsical label; nonetheless, it is thanks to it that we have gotten away with so much. Our nonobservance of the literary ritual could still be tolerated: several rebellious minds could be satisfied, while art was being served just as well as ever. But no one will learn without a shrug of the shoulders that we have agreed to bow to an even more imbecilic formality, which it will be time to specify later on; we will see that carrying out this formality is necessary for anyone who wishes to monitor our results. I fully expect that, after reading this, many will deem with relief that "poetry" has nothing to lose by it: its account is squared.

To a certain degree it is generally known what my friends and I mean by *Surrealism.* We use this word, which we did not coin and which we might easily have left to the most ill-defined critical vocabulary, in a precise sense. This is how we have agreed to designate a certain psychic automatism that corresponds rather well to the dream state, a state that it is currently very hard to delimit. I apologize for introducing a personal observation at this point.

In 1919 my attention had been drawn to the phrases of varying length that, in complete solitude, as I was falling asleep, became perceptible to my mind, without my being able to find anything that might have predetermined them. These sentences, which were syntactically correct and remarkably rich in images, struck me as poetic elements of the first rank. At first I did no more than jot them down. Only later did Soupault and I think of voluntarily re-creating in ourselves the state in which they took form. All we had to do was shut out the external world, and so it was that they occurred to us for two months running, increasingly plentiful, soon following each other without pause and with such speed that *we had to resort to abbreviations* in order to get them all on paper. The book *The Magnetic Fields* is but the first application of that discovery: each chapter had no other reason for stopping than the end of the day on which it was composed, and from one chapter to the next, only a change in velocity caused its slight variations in effect. What I am saying here, without any concern for ridicule or self-promotion, tends mainly to establish that in the absence of any critical intervention on our parts, the judgments to which the publication of such a book might expose us fall by the wayside a priori. Nonetheless, by heeding voices other than that of our own unconscious, even in fun, we risked compromising this self-sufficient murmur in its essence, and I believe that this is ultimately what happened. Nevermore after this, on the occasions when we awaited this murmur in hopes of capturing it for precise ends, did it take us very far. And yet such had been its power that I expect nothing else to afford a greater revelation. I have never lost my conviction that nothing said or done is worthwhile outside obedience to that magic *dictation*. That is the secret of the irresistible attraction that certain individuals exert on us, whose only interest is to have once made themselves the echo of what we are tempted to consider the universal consciousness — or, if you prefer, to have gathered (without necessarily grasping their meaning) a few words fallen from the "mouth of shadows."

It is true that I occasionally refer to a different viewpoint, and this because, as I see it, all human effort must be applied toward recapturing that earlier confidence. All we can do is stand before it without fear of losing our way. It is a crazy man indeed who, having once approached it, brags of having been able to hold onto it. Only those who are well versed in the most complex mental gymnastics have even a chance of possessing it now and again. Today these individuals are named Picabia and Duchamp. Each time this confidence comes forward, almost always unexpectedly, the trick is to know how to receive it without hope of turning back, by attaching only the most relative importance to the form it has taken in announcing its presence.

Getting back to "Surrealism," I had recently decided that the incursions of conscious elements in this domain, which would place it under a well-determined human or literary will, would subject it to the sort of exploitation that could bear only less and less fruit. I would soon lose all interest in it. Along these same lines, I had come to devote my preference to *dream narratives,* which I planned to have taken down stenographically to avoid similar stylization. The problem was that this new test required the help of memory, which is profoundly deficient and, generally speaking, not very reliable. It seemed to me that the matter would go no further, especially owing to the lack of sufficient characteristic documentation. This is why I had stopped expecting much of anything in this regard when a third solution to the problem arose (I believe all that remains is to decipher it), a solution that offers infinitely fewer causes for error and is therefore extremely exciting. You can judge by the fact that after ten days the most blasé, the most self-assured among us stand confused, trembling with gratitude and fear.

Two weeks ago, on his return from holidays, René Crevel described to us the beginnings of a "spiritualist" initiation that he had had thanks to a certain Madame D. This person, having discerned particular mediumistic qualities in him, had taught him how to develop these qualities; so it was that, in the conditions necessary for the production of such phenomena (darkness and silence in the room, a "chain" of hands around the table), he had soon fallen asleep and uttered words that were organized into a generally coherent discourse, to which the usual awakening techniques put a stop at a given moment. It goes without saying that at no time, starting with the day we agreed to try these experiments, have we ever adopted the spiritualist viewpoint. As far as I'm concerned, I absolutely refuse to admit that any communication whatsoever can exist between the living and the dead.

On Monday, 25 September, at 9:00 P.M., in the presence of Desnos, Morise, and myself, Crevel enters into a hypnotic slumber and utters a kind of defense or indictment that was not copied down at the time (declamatory diction interspersed with sighs, sometimes going into a kind of singsong; stressing of certain words, rapid slurring of others; infinite prolongation of several endings; dramatic delivery: the story concerns a woman accused of having killed her husband, but her guilt is in dispute because she apparently acted on his wishes). Upon awakening, Crevel

has no recollection of his words. We exclude him from the following experiment, undertaken, aside from his participation, in
the same conditions. No immediate result. After fifteen minutes,
Desnos—who considered himself the least prone to such demonstrations, fortified in his opinion by the defeat he had inflicted
in my company several days before on two public hypnotists,
Messrs. Donato and Bénévol—lets his head drop onto his arms
and begins compulsively scratching the tabletop. He wakes up of
his own accord several moments later, convinced that he has behaved no differently from the rest of us. To persuade him of his
error, we must separately describe in writing what took place.

Crevel having told us that the action of scratching the table
might indicate a desire to write, it is agreed that the next time
we will place a pencil in Desnos's hand and a sheet of paper in
front of him. So it is that two days later, in similar circumstances,
we see him write before our eyes, without moving his head, the
words *14 July–14 Jul* littered with "+" signs or crosses. At that
point we begin questioning him:

> *What do you see?*
> *Death.*
> He draws a hanged woman at the side of a path.
> Written: *Near the fern go two* (the rest is lost on the tabletop).
> At that moment, I place my hand over his left hand.
> Q: *Desnos, it's Breton here. Tell us what you see for him.*
> A: *The equator* (he draws a circle and a horizontal diameter).
> Q: *Is this a trip Breton will take?*
> A: *Yes.*
> Q: *Will it be a business trip?*
> A: (He shakes his head. Writes:) *Nazimova.*
> Q: *Will his wife travel with him?*
> A: ????
> Q: *Will he go to find Nazimova?*
> A: *No* (underlined).
> Q: *Will he be with Nazimova?*
> A: ?
> Q: *What else do you know about Breton? Speak.*

A: *The boat and the snow—there is also the pretty telegraph tower—on the pretty tower there is a young* (illegible).

I take my hand away. Eluard puts his in its place.

Q: *It's Eluard.*

A: *Yes.* (Drawing.)

Q: *What do you know about him?*

A: *Chirico.*

Q: *Will he soon meet Chirico?*

A: *Marvel with soft eyes like a young baby.*

Q: *What do you see of Eluard?*

A: *He is blue.*

Q: *Why is he blue?*

A: *Because the sky is nesting in* (an unfinished, indecipherable word; the whole sentence is furiously crossed out).

Péret's hand replaces Eluard's.

Q: *What do you know about Péret?*

A: *He will die in a crowded train car.*

Q: *Will he be killed?*

A: *Yes.*

Q: *By whom?*

A: (He draws a train, with a man falling from its door.) *By an animal.*

Q: *By what animal?*

A: *A blue ribbon my sweet vagabond.*

Long pause, then: *Say no more about her, she will be born in a few minutes.*

Ernst's hand replaces Péret's.

Q: *This is Ernst's hand. Do you know him?*

A: *Who?*

Q: *Max Ernst.*

A: *Yes.*

Q: *Will he live long?*

A: *Fifty-one years.*

Q: *What will he do?*

A: *He'll play with madmen.*

Q: *Will these madmen make him happy?*

A: *Ask that blue woman.*
Q: *Who is that blue woman?*
A: THE.
Q: *The? What?*
A: *The tower*

We put an end to Desnos's slumber. Sudden awakening preceded by violent movements.

It should be noted that on the same day, before Desnos, Crevel passed through a state similar to Monday's (another crime story, although more obscure this time: "The woman will be naked, and it's the oldest man who will wield the ax").

During a third attempt, in the presence of Eluard, Ernst, Morise, Péret, a young woman named Mlle Renée who came with Péret, and myself, Mlle Renée is the first to fall asleep. She immediately shows signs of great agitation and calls out breathless phrases. She answers our questions: "The abyss . . . the clear sweat of my father is soaking me!" (repetitions, signs of terror).

A final attempt results, after several minutes, in a loud, sudden, and very lengthy guffaw from Péret. Is he asleep? With great pains we finally extract a few words from him.

What do you see?
Water.
What color is this water?

Same answer. As if it were obvious.

He abruptly stands without being asked, flops belly down on the table, and makes swimming motions.

I think it would be boring to say any more about the particulars of each phenomenon and the circumstances in which we witnessed it: we being Eluard, Ernst, Morise, and I, who despite all our goodwill, did not manage to fall asleep.

Francis Picabia

You don't lend anything to Francis Picabia, not because he is not the richest man in the world,[1] but because any commentary on his work would seem tacked on and could be considered only an act of incomprehension. All Picabia's activity ardently opposes such an addition. Doesn't correcting oneself, just as much as repeating oneself, mean undermining the only chance one has at every minute of lasting beyond one's time? You have not stopped running, and whatever distance you think you've put between you and yourself, you constantly leave new pillars of salt behind on your path. Will you be the only one never to feel that your heart isn't in it? And let no one object that Picabia has to die someday; it's enough that at this moment the very idea strikes me as insane.

I am young enough still to be amazed—need I add that I'm rather pleased with myself over this?—at not finding Picabia to be the all-powerful head of an international mission whose goals (not easily defined, moreover) would strangely surpass those of poetry or painting. It's not just that we are increasingly prey to boredom and that, if we are not careful, "that delicate monster"[2] will soon make us lose interest in anything whatsoever—in other words, will deprive us of every reason to live. Picabia's example is uncommonly useful in this regard. Someone was telling me that in New York, among the visitors who flock to art gallery openings, there are always a few who cast a disenchanted eye at the wall and quickly ask about the next artist to be shown. If by

1. A reference to the common expression "One lends only to the rich." (trans.)

2. The image is from Baudelaire's liminary poem "To the Reader," in *Les Fleurs du Mal.* (trans.)

some impossibility this were to happen at one of Picabia's shows, I would like the answer simply to be Francis Picabia. So true is it that in such things we can benefit only from change, and the man who provides the greatest change from Picabia is Picabia.

We need to open our eyes wide to take in that huge landscape, and in so doing, the emotion of *something never seen* hardly leaves us time to breathe. The forward movement calculated according to its articulations in view of new forward movements; a thought that responds to no known necessity other than the faith in its own exception; the perpetual security in insecurity that confers on it the dangerous element, without which it would in turn run the risk of becoming pedagogical; the humor, inaccessible to women, which, even beyond poetry, is what can best stand in opposition to any mobilization, be it military, artistic, or even "Dada"—which in itself is amusing (both the humor and the *scandal* it entails); every talent, too, including the secret of deriving no particular delight from these talents, like luck in gambling; love above all, tireless love, whose very language the books *Cinquante-deux miroirs* and *Poésie ronron* have borrowed and whose charming machinations they have espoused—all these mean that there are a few of us who, every morning on awakening, wish we could consult Picabia like a marvelous barometer on the atmospheric changes that took place overnight.

For many, this night is total, and I do not expect the following anecdote to have any special impact. But I heard it from Picabia, and in the context of these lives, it warrants being taken for a shaft of light: One day a friend of his, Mr. S. S., of high Persian nobility, had gone to see an art exhibit in Lausanne, after which the young man, who had fortunately remained alien to our "culture," said, "Really, all these artists are just beginners; they're still copying apples and melons and jam jars" and, at the remark that it was beautifully painted, "The truly beautiful thing is to paint an *invention* well. This gentleman—Cézanne, as you call him—has the mind of a greengrocer."

The truth is that we sought the reason for these exercises in vain. It is no harder to make a good painting than it is to make a good meal, if one follows the recipe. A recent experiment has shown that a given individual, under hypnosis, is capable of excelling in the most difficult genre, provided that it be a defined genre to which the subject's attention has previously been drawn. The famous maxim "To understand is to equal" should thus be taken in the strict sense. No need to look any further to understand the success of this or that artistic formula, at whose origin one never finds anything more than a convention. We have become used to legitimizing such conventions by invoking the *need for harmony*. The word *harmony* is absolutely devoid of meaning and evinces no more than the desire to express retroactively, and completely unsatisfactorily, the fact that we experience only reasonable emotions, which matters hardly at all. Hence the long-standing preference for fixed forms in literature; hence the dogma of "composition" in painting. Only at the price of a constant renewal, particularly of means, can an artist avoid becoming prisoner of a genre that he might or might not have created.

And if one is irrevocably wedded to harmony, wouldn't one be justified in speaking of it in relation to the watercolors that Picabia is exhibiting in November 1922 (the oldest of which dates back only a few months) or in invoking any other mystical hypothesis? If such laws existed, I think they would not be appropriate for optics and that they would indicate no production so strongly as this one. The work of art no longer resides in a more or less fortunate assemblage of colors, in a play of lines that more or less touches fingers with reality. Likeness, even a distant one, no longer exists. The farce of interpretation has lasted far too long. The grace of known contours, in which Picabia has so often painted beautiful Spanish women, and the romance of tones to which he has given this tragic turn—he who was the first to paint a blue earth and a red sky—yield to compositions in which visual values, unadulterated by any representative or symbolic intent, are no more significant than the signature and the title. Remember that it was Picabia who once entitled some circles *Ecclesiastic* [*Edtaonisl*] and a straight line, *Star Dancer*. What I find a bit regrettable about this procedure, which nonetheless derives from one of the finest idealistic discoveries I know, is that it too systematically counts on the amazement of spectators, who are always ready to believe that they're being taken for a ride. Here that drawback is no longer at issue, since none of these titles allows for either images or double meanings. It is impossible to see them as anything other than a necessary complement to the rest of the painting. Given the spirit in which these paintings were conceived, and after having stressed Picabia's first-rate faculty for breaking with the images that others would have been pleased to leave of themselves, is it really necessary to point out that we would be wrong to try to include these latest works in his "mechanical period"? It would be a veritable confusion, and I see no need to contest so superficial a judgment.

But what objections we have to face! Another painter who is, alongside Picabia and Duchamp, no doubt the man to whom we owe the most—Picasso—told me the other day that, seeing a painting of his in which he had left areas of bare canvas exposed (figuring that the absence of color was still a color), his friends were unanimous in deploring that the work remained unfinished. He was forced to tell them that the white areas of the canvas had been painted *by his hand*. Given that, how can we expect those who comment on Picabia's watercolors not to incriminate the distribution of colored elements on the paper, the moving appearance of chemical disjunction that some of them give, which up until now we considered to be the very opposite of a painterly arrangement? And how can most people see that, for the first time, a form of painting has become a source of mystery, after having for so long been only speculation about mystery, and that with this art without models, which is neither decorative nor symbolic, Picabia has probably reached the highest rung on the ladder of creation?

Words without Wrinkles

We were beginning to distrust words; we were suddenly noticing that they had to be treated other than as the little auxiliaries
for which they had always been taken. Some thought that they
had become worn down from having served so much; others,
that by their essence they could legitimately aspire to a condition
other than the one they had—in short, we had to free them. The
"alchemy of the verb" had been superseded by a veritable chemistry that first and foremost had put its energies into disengaging
the properties of these words; of these properties, only one—
meaning—was specified by the dictionary. It was a matter (1) of
considering the word in itself and (2) of examining as closely as
possible the reactions words could have to each other. Only at
this price could we hope to restore language's true destination,
which for some (myself included) promised to take knowledge a
giant leap forward, and exalt life by as much. We thereby lay ourselves open to the usual persecutions in a domain where good
(good usage) consists mainly in remembering the etymologies
of words, in other words, their deadest weight, and in making
the sentence conform to a mediocre and utilitarian syntax, where
everything is in agreement with paltry human conservatism and
with a loathing of the infinite that never wastes an opportunity
to show its face. Naturally such an enterprise, which is part of the
poetic impulse, does not demand so much clear will from each
of those who take part in it; one does not always have to formulate a need in order to satisfy it. And my intent here is only to
develop an image.

It was by assigning color to vowels that for the first time,
consciously and in full knowledge of the consequences, some-

one turned the word away from its duty to signify. That day it emerged into concrete existence, such as no one had ever suspected it might have. There is no point in debating the exactness of the phenomenon of colored audition, on which I will be sure not to rely. The important thing is that the alarm has been sounded and that from now on it seems imprudent to speculate about the innocence of words. We now know that, all in all, they have a sonority that is sometimes quite complex; moreover, they have tempted painter's brushes, and very soon we will be studying their architectural side. This is a small, intractable world over which we can float only the most insufficient surveillance balloons and in which, even so, we occasionally spot some flagrant violations. In fact, the expression of an idea depends as much on a word's aspect as on its meaning. There are words that work against the idea they are claiming to express. Indeed, even the meaning of words is not always pure, and we are nowhere near determining to what degree the figurative sense progressively acts on the literal sense, each variation in the latter supposedly entailing a variation in the former.

In this regard today's poetry offers a unique field of observation. The names Paulhan, Eluard, and Picabia are linked to research in which the works of Ducasse, Mallarmé's *Un Coup de dés,* and Apollinaire's "Victory" and certain other calligrams also have a hand. Still, we were not certain that words were already living their own life; we did not dare see them as creators of energy. We had emptied them of their thought and were waiting, in no real anticipation, for them to command thought. But now it has come to pass: they are doing what we expected of them. The document that proves it is, in many respects, invaluable.

Of course, the six "word games" published in the next-to-last issue of *Littérature* and signed Rrose Sélavy seemed to me to warrant the closest possible attention, and this without regard for the personality of the author, Marcel Duchamp, but because of these two discrete aspects: on the one hand, their mathematical rigor (the displacement of a letter within a word, exchange of syllables between two or more words, etc.); on the other, the absence of the comic element, which was considered endemic to the genre and was enough to ruin it. To my mind it was the most remarkable thing to happen in poetry in a long time. Still, Robert Desnos and I could not have foreseen back then that a new problem would attach itself to this one, thereby bringing it to the front line of current concerns. Who dictates to a *sleeping* Desnos the sentences that can be read in *Littérature,* sentences in which Rrose Sélavy is again the heroine? Is Desnos's brain linked (as he claims) to Duchamp's, to the point where Rrose Sélavy speaks to him only if Duchamp is wide awake? In the current state of affairs, this is not up to me to elucidate. I should point out only that, awake, Desnos has proven incapable—like the rest of us—of pursuing this series of "word games," even after long effort. For nearly a month, moreover, our friend has been sparing us no surprise, and I have seen from his hand (he who, in his normal state, does not know how to draw) a series of sketches, including one called *The City with Nameless Streets of the Cerebral Circus,* about which I will simply say for the moment that they move me more than anything else.

I ask the reader to be content for now with this initial evidence of an activity that we had never suspected. Several of us attach extreme importance to it. And let it be quite understood that when we say "word games," it is our surest reasons for living that are being put into play. Words, furthermore, have finished playing games.

Words are making love.

Distance

The visual arts, beginning with painting, which more than all the others in the nineteenth century evidenced a coherent, sustained effort, in perfect harmony with the spirit that guided and, I would even say, generated that period—the visual arts have in the past few years been undergoing a crisis that requires definition.

On the eve of the last war the most independent art critics could have been proud of their successes. The greatest spoils went to those who could best rehabilitate the damned: Delacroix, Corot, Courbet, Manet, and Cézanne. At the same time they were falling over each other in their efforts to condemn official art, charged with being the root of all evil. The words "acquired by the State," "medal of honor," or even "sold" at the bottom of a painting seemed enough to discredit its author forever. Public opinion, so well behaved, had itself taken to the game, and artists no longer knew where to turn so as not to prove unworthy of this amiable posterity before the fact. Although the fruits of a rather vulgar anticipation might not always have been succulent, anything was better, we were assured, than the products of a routine that, after some pathetic misadventures, could no longer claim the label of tradition.

That is where things stood when it was deemed advisable to inflict on us the harsh lesson of 1914, '15, '16, '17, and '18. Under the weight of what those years offered by way of nostalgia, repressed pride, and permanent disuse of the faculty of choice (to put this in the minor key), the will to modernism, which until then had enjoyed free rein, slowly collapsed. In the realm of the mind—the only one that matters—and despite a few excesses that it repudiated, this will at least appeared fully armed in the face of death. I can judge at leisure, having for a time bent my own will to that magnificent slavery. I am saying this to indicate, first and foremost, that painting (for instance) cannot take visual pleasure as its goal and that I find the Epicurean morality, which military events have made fashionable again, totally inapplicable. I persist in thinking that a painting or piece of sculpture can be conceived only secondarily from the viewpoint of taste and holds its own only insofar as it is liable to take our abstract knowledge, properly speaking, a step forward.

What makes me fear that the quasi totality of current artistic production does not deserve the increasing attention being paid it is that for the past five years it has stopped being a part of that disquiet whose only flaw was to become systematic. Critics tried in vain to guide us through that sea of oil: some, all the while feeding us glimpses of the Renaissance pavillion, underhandedly drag us to the depths of time's abyss, misrecognizing (and for good reason) the barbarity of life; others, prostrated on their youth, ask a few illustrious survivors for more than they can still give. None of them, by mutual agreement, bothers to make any sort of distinction among the new works, so that only the painter's *craft* still matters, and we consequently find more nonentities to exert this craft with each passing day.

So as to deal the death blow to one of the most admirable means of expression I know, financial speculation got into the game, and they're now monitoring artistic changes as rigorously as they do the monetary exchange.[1] Art is being liquidated the same as nations. Here again, criticism is no longer up to the task. Long jealous of the apparent sanction conferred on its judgments by the noisy announcement of certain sale prices, criticism now seems to be no more than the shifty agent of these transactions, which have nothing whatsoever to do with art but which still threaten to devalue it. Whatever the plane on which one might situate the artistic products we are shown, and even if it's a mat-

1. Untranslatable pun on the word *change,* which can mean either "change" or, in a financial context, "exchange." (trans.)

ter of only one work out of ten or one hundred, I see no way to keep silent about such a grave danger. Art is, I repeat, currently under the sway of dealers, and this to the great shame of artists.

It is already unfortunate that so few opportunities exist for a painter to bring his work to public attention, apart from art galleries. His presence in those evil places almost always leads him to make compromises that I am not prepared to forgive. I do not understand how someone who loves painting can stand to make the rounds of exhibits every week, and still less how he usually looks no further than that. Of course there are the salons, or rather the Salon, for we know from experience that we can expect nothing from the official juries. But even the Salon des Indépendants is showing signs of fatigue. Several of the artists we are interested in have abandoned it entirely. Certain regulations, no different from any others, are beginning to take hold in it. Finally, the particular viewpoint that reigns in the Indépendants favors only the discovery of works that are often unable to bear up under my own "lights," which are not, and by a long stretch, those of the Grand Palais.[2]

Alongside the material difficulties that, as I see it, the visual arts—which moreover are more materially bound than the other arts—are experiencing, we should also, to explain their current state of crisis, take into account a fundamental misunderstanding. The visual arts have always claimed certain perspectives that, incidentally, it would not be inappropriate to challenge. Under the pretext that the manual labor that painters and sculptors are called on to perform sets them apart from the poet and musician (and we know that no prejudice is more firmly rooted; the social problem rests in part on this sort of assumption), it is almost always with a sly air that the author of a canvas or monument suffers the comments that those who "are not in the art world" feel entitled to make about his work. Eighty percent of the time noth-

2. The 1923 Salon des Indépendants had been held from 10 February through 11 March. Many painters had abstained from exhibiting, discouraged by the poor lighting in the Grand Palais and the principle by which works were arranged: in alphabetical order by artist's name. (trans.)

ing can annoy him more than to have someone ascribe intentions to him other than strictly animal instinct. For him, the ideal is to make people say, like Renoir, that he considered a "nude" finished when he wanted to feel up her behind. I would be all in favor of this sensuality if it did not tell us far too much about the quality of the painter's ambitions. I persist in thinking that we can expect more interesting revelations from painting, and I am astounded to find, in the incomprehensible disdain of everything having to do with thought, the true causes of the current violent reaction against the well- or ill-inspired representatives of the opposite tendency: Gustave Moreau, Gauguin, Seurat, Redon, Picasso. It is hardly my intention to place all modern painting under the banner of these names. Just let me say that if we were to be influenced by that rather than by something else, we would not be where we are today: perhaps we would eat fewer apples and would not be forced to endure the proximity of that woman whom we have not invited and whom we are tired of seeing lounging in more or less suggestive poses on our sofa.

It is pointless to distinguish between "literary" painting and painting proper, as some maliciously persist in doing. Moreover, as can never be said too often, there can be no bestial art. To lapse into decoration (and all things considered, decoration of what?) is no solution, either. This is nonetheless the fate of much overly formal research today, which is enough to condemn it. Cubism, which for a moment dominated the situation, is dying at the hands of its exegetes, who for lack of being able to elevate the discussion are reducing it to the proportion of a technical apprenticeship. Mediocrity is taking advantage of the situation to reinstate itself pretty much everywhere.

Does this mean that the situation is hopeless? We should guard against making dire predictions for the future on the basis of these summary observations. Let's not forget that, when on the verge of revealing some of its noblest secrets, the world often makes a great and weary gesture that does nothing to halt the impenitent march of the latest conqueror.

Characteristics of the
Modern Evolution and
What It Consists Of

GENTLEMEN,

Nonchalance, when it travels abroad, relinquishes most of its prerogatives; otherwise—although I have given little thought to the proper form for a lecture—I would probably behave quite differently with you. As a rule I believe that a critical study is not appropriate in these circumstances and that the smallest theatrical effect would convey my message much more clearly. Alfred Jarry seated at a rickety table next to the curtain at the premiere of *Ubu Rex,* a glass of absinthe within reach, staring vacantly at the audience of the Théâtre de l'Oeuvre; or Arthur Cravan in New York during the war, once a crowd had shown up at the Independents' exhibit to hear him lecture on modern humor, lurching onstage to emit only hiccups and to start undressing before an outraged public, until the police cut short his performance: these are the examples I would have kept in mind had I been speaking anywhere else. All in all a sense of provocation is still the most noticeable thing in this domain; a truth will always benefit from adopting an outrageous means of expression. In my case I am not possessed by the desire to impose my point of view, whatever it may be; indeed, I hold it only as long as I have not yet managed to make others share it. It is at this price that those I love and I are hoping to maintain a certain aristocracy of thought, which is the only means by which we might perhaps be induced to "return to tradition"[1]—about which, furthermore, we couldn't care less, given that this tradition, if there is one, proceeds by astonishing fits and starts and proves in its choices to

1. A major aesthetic preoccupation in the years immediately after the war. See Breton's remarks in the essay "Distance." (trans.)

be infinitely less rigid and stubborn than the swine who speak in its name.

But I repeat, we are in Barcelona, and my perfect ignorance of Spanish culture, Spanish desire, a cathedral under construction[2] that I rather like if I forget that it is a cathedral, your climate, and the women I pass on the street who are so delightfully foreign to me have somewhat undermined my natural audacity. I cannot put a name to a single one of your faces, gentlemen, and so I momentarily believe we have a good chance of understanding each other. You probably have no reason to distrust me, and to show you that I'd like to put my best foot forward, I will add that, since you are artists, there might well be among you a great artist or, who knows, a man of the kind I admire who, behind the noise of my words, will distinguish a current of ideas and sensations not very different from his own. I say "ideas and sensations" because I myself operate in a world in which sensations have more weight than ideas, emanate in a certain way from ideas, in the same way that ideas proceed (or so they've taught us) from elementary sensations. I count much more on the communication of these sensations than on the persuasive virtues of ideas. Moreover, I put great stock in the impenetrable curiosity that, on the intellectual plane, sometimes leads a country to welcome the first foreign viewpoint to come along. All this allows me to embroil myself no further in these preambles. And I send greetings from here to my good friend Francis Picabia, who is in the audience— Picabia, who would like to remain unmoved but whose heart is nonetheless a bit too attached to this region, which he tells me is the Ireland of Spain, a region that I rather believe that a man we both love, Pablo Picasso, also remembers fondly.

These days there are several individuals prowling over the world for whom art, for example, has ceased to be an end in itself. (To

2. Antonio Gaudí's Sagrada Familia, which Breton discovered and admired during this visit to Barcelona—so much so that he sent a view of it to Picasso soon after his arrival, asking the painter whether he was "familiar with this marvel." (trans.)

forestall uncertainties, I intend from the start to avoid any artistic debates.) It is quite understood that not one of them has any intention of beautifying someone else's leisure time in even the slightest way. If they have taken a stand with artists, and have therefore been discussed in the same breath, this does not mean that art is their only mode of expression. This race of men is not about to die out and must show what it can do in every sphere of activity. The day will come when we approach even the sciences in this poetic spirit, which at first glance seems so contrary to them. In some ways it is the genius of *invention* that is breaking its fetters and preparing to wreak its gentle havoc from all sides. I do not say these things lightly, and I can answer the objection that some of you gentlemen will no doubt make: "You have been taken in by a mirage," you'll tell me; "your dream, which is as old as the world, is to go knock at the gates of creation, at which many before you have fallen. Your great trick is to scatter over that no-man's-land into which your Apollinaire and a few others have already tried to drag us. And what did Apollinaire finally manage to say about that modern spirit that he spent his time preaching? Just read the article that appeared a few days before his death, 'The New Spirit and the Poets,' to realize the nothingness of his meditation and the pointlessness of all that noise." Excuse me, gentlemen, if I have gone beyond your thinking. If the minds of a few harbingers contained more blind faith than poignant lucidity—which is undeniable—this hardly eliminates the problem. Each of you knows that a body of work such as Rimbaud's does not end, as the schoolbooks tell us, in 1875 and that one would be mistaken in believing that one could penetrate its meaning without following the poet all the way to his death. This work, which revolutionized poetry (I'm not saying anything new), should remain on our path as a guiding light. In this regard it is seconded by the work of another great poet, unfortunately all but unknown, Germain Nouveau, who early on renounced even his own name and took to begging. The reason for such an attitude strangely defies words, that is certain, but wasn't it the same for the Sphinx, whose question was nonetheless unavoidable?

Yes, it is indeed the inevitability of this question that weighs over us, and as we examine the men and ideas that I intend to speak about this evening, we will find ourselves confronted over and over by this same question, which will vary only in intensity. In this regard I should point out that Rimbaud did nothing more than to express, with surprising vigor, a malaise that probably thousands of generations before him had not managed to avoid and to give it a voice that still sounds in our ears. Before getting to him, we believe we have overheard at very rare intervals—in a scientist's complaint, a criminal's defense, or a philosopher's distraction—an awareness of that terrifying duality that is the marvelous wound on which he put his finger. But each time it was just an alarm; immediately the abyss closed up again and the world returned for another century to its childish scaffoldings and obvious subterfuges.

Are we even a little bit free? Will we at least reach the end of the path that we see our actions taking, which is so beautiful when one stops to look at it? Isn't this path an optical illusion? Why were we made and what can we accept being made for? Must we abandon all hope?

From this anxiety comes the question that concerns us, a question that is all the more anxiety laden in that we are given our whole lives to reflect on it and that even if we somehow managed to answer it, we would die all the same.

It was in the wake of such considerations that I had thought to organize a Congress of Paris last summer, devoted to the so-called modern spirit, during which I had hoped to verify an idea that had occurred to me—an insane idea, as you will see, but one that I was weak enough to cherish. Via a great number of productions—some utterly devoid of personality, others that seemed to me as unworthy as could be—with which the book and painting industries flood us every day, I believed I could discern some basic statements common to all of them, and I was anxious to clarify for myself some kind of tendency. Perhaps a poor outcome did not necessarily imply a fundamental indigence; perhaps all these brains were possessed by the same desire and would benefit on this score from no longer being so in the dark about themselves. You can judge how naive I was. After having been refused several times (André Gide disdained to participate in a congress whose aim, he said, was to teach people how to mass produce works of art), I had managed as best I could to convince a representative from each of the five or six active groups (so-called) to join me in trying to realize my project. From a confrontation of modern values, to use the terminology of certain of my collaborators, we were ultimately seeking a great spark. We were soon forced to lower our sights. Preparations for the congress were endless, on top of which the astonishing vanity of each of its members conspired to make everything impossible. And to top it off, Mr. Tristan Tzara, who did not find any personal benefit in all this and whose head, as usual, had been turned by a few press clippings, deemed it worth his while to gain an upper hand over the congress that I saw no point in challenging.

I was cured of my illusion, quite resolved from then on not to tempt my intellectual fate in such precarious byways. Without wishing to bring the debate onto the terrain of sincerity, we must admit that by a singular change of affairs it is now more lucrative to pass for an independent than to solicit official rewards. With the worst bad faith in the world, my friends and I have been accused of trying to revive so-called accursed poetry [*poésie maudite*]. Aside from the fact that this expression already strikes me as deplorable when applied to those for whom it was invented (we could expect no better from Verlaine, whom we gladly leave, along with Albert Samain, to little girls in the provinces), we must recognize that if this were our aim, we would be going about it rather badly. If one could still speak of "accursed poetry," it would be in reference to academic verse, for which, as you know, we have no taste whatsoever. It is bad enough that the most asinine simulation of intellectual originality enjoys widespread acclaim these days. No, I am not demanding the romantic privilege of exile for artists or individuals. But I wanted to stress that, in our day and age, it is impossible to conceive of "accursed poetry," for this would immediately ensure its public acceptance and by that very token stop it from being accursed. The point of this long aside, gentlemen, is to help you to understand why I am avoiding using the words *modern spirit* to designate the body of research that concerns us—that is, the only research worth considering. These words have been much bandied about in recent times, very often as a cover for opportunism, which is too nauseating for me to say any more about it. If you want proof, you have only to leaf through *Les Feuilles libres* or *La Vie des lettres*. At the present time it would be more imprudent than ever to risk making long generalizations on the subject. Its only effect would be to aggravate the misunderstanding that I forced myself to give you an idea of earlier. I believe that it is better not to waste any more time affirming a cause shared by many and to stick with juxtaposing, as I propose to do here, several particularly typical wills, mainly chosen from among those for whom I can answer and whom I have gathered together with the sole aim of revealing in its broad lines the evolution taking place in France, as it has appeared to me since the not-so-distant day when I first got wind of it.

And first of all, a few words about the movements that have succeeded each other since Symbolism and Impressionism, on which I have only historical data, not having been present even for their decline. Much ill has been said of schools, and it is often repeated that "genius" owes them nothing. The word *school* would already be tendentious if we did not know that with distance it is impossible to appreciate what kind of life passed through an insurrection or, even more so, an intellectual movement. I'm thinking of this poem by Charles Cros, a true innovator, that contains these lines:

> *But I am very much alive: the coming wind brings*
> *A scent of flowering hawthorn and lilac.*
> *The sound of my kisses hides the tolling bell.*

These lines might have been written in an admirable fervor; it is rather sad to note that today they are no more than poor verses. It's just that the same mask covers men's thoughts and their faces in death. The enthusiasm is gone, and who could recapture it now? Still, each of the movements we are speaking of must have corresponded to a reality since lost. What we can know of the nineteenth century in France only reinforces this opinion. If it was not movements that made men, it is still pretty rare for the most remarkable among them not to have been aligned with one. There is a strength in them—a rather mysterious one, moreover—outside of which I see no salvation for the mind in a given time period. And let no one object that this apparent concession to one's times undermines the durable influence an individual might wield. The case of Stendhal attests to the contrary: too few people know that Stendhal was the author of a Romantic treatise that was just as fiery as any other. And it is also to Romanticism that the two poets I would link to the two principal currents of contemporary poetry were attached: on the one hand, Aloysius Bertrand, who, via Baudelaire and Rimbaud, leads to Reverdy; on the other, Gérard de Nerval, whose soul glides from Mallarmé through Apollinaire to reach us.

It is likely, therefore, that the history of the most recent intellectual movements would involve the most notorious personalities of our time. Still, while there is reason to mark three successive stages in this history, I believe not that Cubism, Futurism, and Dada are, all things considered, three distinct movements but rather that all three are part of a more general movement whose meaning and scope we do not yet fully know. To tell the truth, Futurism is not nearly as interesting as the two others, and to fit it into this account we should look only at its intentions. But to study Cubism, Futurism, and Dada successively is to follow the thrust of an idea that has now reached a certain height and that is awaiting only a new impetus to continue describing its assigned arc.

One man whose determinations appear to have set everything in motion—for although they might seem to regulate only the fate of painting, they are of crucial interest to thought and life—is certainly Picasso. Let's not forget that the principle of more or less lyrical distortion that Matisse and Derain got, I believe, from African art had hardly freed painting from its representational conventions, with which Picasso was the first to break. The discovery of virgin territory, on which the most sparkling whim can roam freely, is perhaps the first instance of art taking on a certain *outlaw* side, which we will not lose sight of as we go along. This is because, before Picasso, painting seemed to depend much more on available materials than did literature, for example. Someday, perhaps, life itself will stop being subject to what we still consider its practical necessities. That is what the revelation called "Cubism" means to me, and only that; the Cubist doctrine—which can in no way be imputed to Picasso and at which he is, furthermore, the first to smile—otherwise strikes me as mediocre and indefensible.

Stemming from Cubism (if we must), in that they share with Picasso the concept of an art that is more than mere borrowing, even as they refuse to set limits for it, as Picasso's followers have done (which is why they are suspect in the eyes of those same followers), Francis Picabia and Marcel Duchamp, in both their artistic activities and their lives overall, seem to oppose the formation of a new cliché that would make us sink lower than low. Both have this in common, that they move without losing sight of the major elevation point where one idea is equal to any other idea, where stupidity encompasses a certain amount of intelligence, and where emotion takes pleasure in being denied. Our most cherished games, beginning with the illusion of not being alone and consequently being able to create in some useful fashion, are pitilessly mocked by them. But whereas Marcel Duchamp still seems to be pondering an experiment aimed at clarifying the antinomy—which threatens to become horrendous—between reason and the senses (and despite so much intellectualism, it is certain that eroticism, for example, is more relevant than ever), we see Francis Picabia taking on social issues and, from the progressive dryness of the air around us, expecting our disgrace to evaporate in a miraculous fever. It might seem strange to speak this way about two painters, but from where I stand, the activities of Francis Picabia and Marcel Duchamp, which complement each other, seem truly inspired. Their vigilance, which has not faltered for a single instant in the last ten years, has several times prevented the handsome vessel that carries us from foundering. And I am quite sure that, without knowing it, they have in their heads the entire map of a journey that they are nonetheless unable to unfold completely and of which they can foresee no more than the coming hour.

Understand me: this is no longer about painting; at most painting forms part of the slipstream, as would a bird's song. We can easily see, then, how illogical it would be, in judging the exhibit of Picabia's drawings that opens tomorrow at the Dalmau gallery, to call on our habitual reference points. We are dealing here not with painting, or even with the poetry or philosophy of painting, but instead with the internal landscapes of a man who struck out long ago for his own furthest pole.

The ability to situate in time, with the most personal of gifts — and since we must go that way, through the medium of colors or words — the disturbance that in some obscure way we all share has certainly not yet abandoned Giorgio de Chirico. This painter, who lives in Italy and whose latest works, to a not very observant viewer, seem to make concession after concession to the most sterile academicism, holds us under the sway of a promise too moving for us ever to turn away from him with indifference. Indeed, it is to Chirico that we owe the revelation of symbols that preside over our instinctive life and that (we suspected as much) are not the same as in the time of the savages. It is a good thing, now and again, to make room for terror, and I can't help seeing, for example, in the canvases Chirico painted between 1912 and 1914 so many rigid images of the declaration of war. All reservations aside, we find something extremely seductive about the apparatus of prophecy. And for the first time in centuries, Chirico has made us hear the irresistible and unjust voice of the soothsayers.

Max Ernst is now devoting his genius to reconciling two no doubt irreconcilable trends, on each of which modern humor has one foot. Putting each one forward by turns, but nonetheless lean-ing a bit more heavily on the latest one, this young man, too, has spied a kind of panic of intelligence from which he has not failed to draw some singular sparks. He also keeps an eye on the insane, and there is a trace in his work of that rather comical primitivism that makes do with the worst complications, in both their draw-ings and their lives. Finally, he goes on as lengthily as Man Ray, although in an entirely different way, about the new conditions imposed on the visual arts by the introduction of photography, and from it he comes around to an almost total subjectivism that no longer respects even the general concept of the object and re-acts on the very vision we might have of the external world.

Man Ray, after whom we will have finished with the visual arts, might pass above all for a photographer in that he has often chosen to express himself via that modern and, if I may say so, eminently revealing instrument, bromide paper. The mystery of the photographic print is intact in the sense that artistic interpre-tation is reduced to a minimum. If pressed, I will admit that one might take a relative interest in the arrangement of a few fruits on a dining room table, or that one might find a ring of keys beautiful. It is not a reason to paint them, and how grateful I am to Picasso, when he wants to take a rest from painting, for turn-ing tin and scraps of newspaper into small objects for his own amusement! Man Ray, by a process of his own, obtains similar results on a sheet of paper. No doubt this holds the promise of an art that is richer in surprises than painting is, for example. I'm reminded of Marcel Duchamp showing friends a birdcage that, as far as they could see, contained no birds but instead was half-filled with sugar cubes, and asking them to lift the cage, which they were astonished to find so heavy. What they had taken for sugar cubes were in fact little pieces of marble that Duchamp, at great expense, had had cut to his specifications. This trick, for me, is as good as any other—and even as good as nearly all the tricks of art put together. This anecdote sums up rather well the novelty of Man Ray's investigations. In this regard they tend to overlap the strictly poetic investigations we have now come to and offer me a transition fluid enough to make it seem that I thought about it long and hard.

Whereas in painting one could say that these six living men have no predecessors (it would be absurd to speak in their regard of Cézanne, about whom I personally could not care less and whose human attitudes and artistic ambitions, despite what his boosters say, I have always considered imbecillic—almost as imbecillic as the current need to praise him to the skies), it is clear that in poetry we can look much further back to find the first evidence of the spirit that concerns us, the starting point of the evolution whose main traits we are now beginning to see. Already in 1870 Isidore Ducasse, under the pseudonym Comte de Lautréamont, was secretly publishing the *Cantos of Maldoror,* just as he himself has managed to reach us in secrecy. To this man, of whom we possess (as with the Marquis de Sade) only apocryphal portraits,[3] falls perhaps the greatest responsibility for the current state of affairs in poetry, if I can use that expression. "At this moment," he was already writing, "new shivers ripple through the intellectual atmosphere: it is simply a matter of having the courage to look them full in the face." Today the issue has still not changed. For Ducasse, imagination is not that abstract little sister jumping rope in the town square; she is sitting in your lap, and in her eyes you have read your perdition. Listen to her: at first you'll think that she doesn't know what she is saying. She doesn't know anything, and soon, with that little hand on which you've planted a kiss, she will caress hallucinations and sensory disturbances in the shadows. No one knows what she wants; she makes you aware of several other worlds at the same time, until you no longer know how to act in this one. Then everything will be put on a trial that must constantly begin anew. Truth, after Ducasse, no longer has

3. Although this was true at the time Breton wrote these lines, a photograph of Ducasse has since come to light. It was first published in Jacques Lefrère, *Le Visage de Lautréamont* (Paris: Pierre Horay, 1977), and has been reproduced many times since. (trans.)

a right or wrong side: good so nicely brings out evil. And where will we *not* find beauty? "Beautiful as the curve described by a dog running after its master . . . beautiful as a hasty burial . . . beautiful as the chance meeting on a dissecting table of a sewing machine and an umbrella." And as all this still risked bearing fruit where there must be no fruit, Ducasse took the precaution, before dying very young, of providing his first book with a rebuttal, entitled *Poésies,* in which he calls with infinite humor on the sentiment of just measure—as if it were not enough that with him Nietzsche's famous "Everything is permitted" stopped being Platonic, and that he meant to convey that debauchery was still the rule most applicable to the mind.

This said, what would be the point in my speaking at length about Rimbaud, for whom our age seems to have invented the words "public domain"? Today there is fierce competition to stroll over the grounds, admirable though they might be, on which a soul met its defeat—a soul that, like Ducasse's, was not that of just another artist, in other words, a professional. There is no use repeating cries other than the ones everyone has heard: "We are not in the world," and further on,

> *All to war, to vengeance and to terror,*
> *My spirit! Let us turn about in the biting jaws. Ah! vanish,*
> *Republics of this world! Of emperors,*
> *Regiments, colonists, peoples—enough!*

—cries to which, with the claim of making Rimbaud serve their cause, particularly the Catholic cause, a certain number of creeps extend the most hypocritical pardons. To be told that Rimbaud inspired a literary school; that his poetic techniques have been freely borrowed, which today allows even a Cocteau to claim him as a forebear; that the protest of his entire being against everything ultimately served *for that*—this, gentlemen, is enough to make you want to bash your head against the wall.

But a silent young man raising a finger in the invisible atmosphere near me, in whom I recognize the gentle old fellow who, barely three years ago, was still begging at the doors of a church in the south, is asking me to stop my cursing. It's Germain Nouveau, who, on earth, "made a vow," figuring (as Rimbaud's former friend) that simply staying on this earth was not vow enough. Nouveau, who for years lived on five cents of alms a day, did everything in his power to spare us the spectacle of those crazed and useless wanderings that we saw Rimbaud make from country to country and job to job—he, the man from nowhere who would "never have his hand."

Nouveau proposed to counter that discipline to which we are subject, and that Rimbaud desperately fought against his whole life, by voluntarily obeying a much harsher discipline. Little by little the mind tempers itself anew in that asceticism, and life can then regain its enchantment. But under the caress of words (whose harmonious power Nouveau knew how to use better than anyone) subsists a harrowing regret.

> *"Everything makes love." And I would add,*
> *When you say everything makes love,*
> *Even the step with the road,*
> *The baton with the drum.*
>
> . . . .
>
> *Yes, everything makes love under the wings*
> *Of love, as if in its palace:*
> *Even the towers of citadels*
> *With the hail of bullets.*

Although in every respect the two figures who come next, especially the second, strike me as being of lesser stature, I still do not see any way to avoid mentioning them. Alfred Jarry and Guillaume Apollinaire, unlike those previously discussed, behaved like professional writers. If we can possibly excuse Jarry, who usually acted in a spirit of mockery, Apollinaire, on the other hand, can claim no extenuating circumstances in this regard. I'll admit that the cartoon image of Alfred Jarry succumbing under the weight of the character he created still moves me. Ubu remains an admirable creation for whom I would give all your

Shakespeares and Rabelaises. I say this all the more willingly in that last year the critics unanimously decreed the worthlessness of an opus that, they believe, can be contained in a little sixty-page paperback and in an evening at the Théâtre de l'Oeuvre, between two "lovely settings of the 'Chauve-Souris.'"[4] Without a doubt such incidents provide constant reason for Jarry's ghost to come back and take a bow. Let's face it: the Palcontents are not dead yet! And it is not entirely in vain that Alfred Jarry tried to make of Ubu's life a wonderful flourish of ink and alcohol, without which the character would be nothing.

Apollinaire's only interest lies in his appearing rather like the last poet, in the most general sense of the word. Because of this we can study him with curiosity and even let ourselves be charmed a bit by a modulation that we sense is about to end. Everything happens, I repeat, within a few volumes of prose or verse, for in him the man is no more than the artist's valet. I won't go so far as to condemn him for his ridiculous attitude during the war. Apollinaire was able all the same to foresee some of the reasons for the modern evolution, and we should recognize that he always gave new ideas an enthusiastic welcome. The fact that his love of scandal might have led him to defend the most dubious innovations, such as some utterly insignificant onomatopoeic poems to which he attributed great importance toward the end of his life, or that he showed himself to be stupidly fond of erudition and trinkets does not conceal for me the horror that he had of stagnation in any form and particularly in himself, he who at least managed not to spend his life rewriting the same poem over and over and who knew—and this is why we love him—how to

4. An allusion to a recent revival of *Ubu Rex* at the Théâtre Fémina on Avenue des Champs-Elysées. The play was given in the interval between two shows by the popular Chauve-Souris troupe from Moscow, which combined dance, music, and comedy sketches—precisely the kind of theatre that Breton despised. The reference to the Théâtre de l'Oeuvre harkens back to the infamous premiere of *Ubu* in 1896. (trans.)

Lose
But lose genuinely
To make room for discovery

No doubt Apollinaire is still a specialist—in other words, one of those individuals for whom I personally have no use. But I am grateful to him for having demonstrated in his specialty a relative freedom large enough for me to take pleasure in the blatant licentiousness of the *Onze Mille Verges,* as well as in the tone of these opening lines:

The concierge's mother and the concierge will let everyone through
If you're a man you'll come with me tonight
All we need is one guy to watch the main entrance
While the other goes upstairs

Of all the living poets, one who seems to have assumed to the highest degree the distance that Apollinaire so totally lacked, one whose life must be considered the most exempt from the platitudes that are the common coin of literary action (and this can be recognized from the fact that, in his own time, he seems destined for extreme solitude), is Pierre Reverdy. In his work, in which the modern mystery is briefly concentrated, he speaks in undertones of things no one knows; that would be nothing if, with him, the simplest word was not constantly being reborn into an existence so figurative that it becomes lost in the indefinite.

The falling night shuts the door
We are at the edge of the road
In the shadows
Near the stream where everything lies.

It is certain that such an attitude, which up until now has been purely static and contemplative, is not sufficient unto itself. But I think it implies an action that Reverdy—if, as I believe, he is not imprisoned by form—is now in a position to take, to our great thrill.

All these remarks on ideas and men lead me, gentlemen, to present Dada to you as the inevitable explosion resulting from that supercharged atmosphere. The rapid passage of Jacques Vaché through the wartime sky, what he carried within him that was so extraordinarly urgent, the catastrophic haste that made him annihilate himself; the chariot-driving whiplashes of Arthur Cravan, himself buried as we speak in the Bay of Mexico: these, along with the marvelous instability of Picabia and Duchamp, were the harbingers of Dada—which perhaps led us to expect more from it than it was able to give. Dada, its insolent negation, its annoying egalitarianism, the anarchic nature of its protest, its love of scandal for scandal's sake, in short, its whole offensive thrust: I don't have to remind you how willingly I subscribed to it for so long. Only one thing can free us—temporarily, at least—from that hideous cage in which we are struggling, and that thing is revolution, any revolution, as bloody as need be, that still today I am calling for with all my might. Too bad if Dada wasn't that, for you understand that the rest is of no importance to me. It is to that latent revolution that I call each of those whose names I've mentioned tonight. If Dada enlisted men who in this respect were not ready to face any challenge, men who were not made of explosive matter, once again I say, too bad for it. And don't expect me to be kinder than necessary to those among us who, for such paltry glory, donned the uniform of volunteers. It would not be a bad idea to reinstitute the laws of the Terror for things of the mind.

By his own admission Tristan Tzara "would have become a successful adventurer, making subtle gestures, if he had had the physical force and nervous stamina to achieve this one exploit: not to be bored." At the end of 1919 Tzara arrived in Paris somewhat like the Messiah. From the two or three words he uttered, I imagined him to have an extremely rich inner life, and I readily accepted whatever he proposed from then on. It seemed back then that Tzara kept a few machines from that necessary Terror at his disposal. So it was that Picabia, Aragon, Eluard, and I let him do as he liked without asking questions. For the time being Tzara was pure of any compromises. His poetry, which, moreover, showed extraordinary personal resources, was not his least potent weapon. Finally, his entrance cut short all those tired old discussions that wore down the streets of the capital a bit more every day. He made not one conciliatory gesture toward retrograde factions. Well! Yes, Tzara did walk for a time with that defiance in his eye, and yet all that wonderful self-assurance could not bring him to stage a veritable coup d'état. It's just that Tzara, who had eyes for no one, one idle day took it into his head to have some for himself, which means that in the short term he already seems no more than a run-of-the-mill general of the Republic who turned coat and whom suicide awaits on some mistress's grave.[5]

Dada is no more, and this, which is a statement of fact rather than a personal observation, is not good news for the owners of little Montmartre cabarets, who are, as we know, the last guardians of our tradition. Just because Dada is part of my memories does not mean I have the slightest difficulty in moving beyond it: the contrary, gentlemen, would have surprised you. Moreover, nearly all those who played a part in it have already thought better of it, without having changed their spots. As far as I'm concerned, it was impossible for me to remain with Dada, which, as a force turned entirely toward the outside, lost all reason for being the moment it proved powerless to modify the proportions of the conflict. But on this score I am seconded in my bitterness by Richard Huelsenbeck, who deems that our sacrifice was worth more than this and that there was no point in herding us down into streets that lead only to false "new arrivals" shelves in the neighborhood bookstore and drinks in cafés.

Philippe Soupault is the only one at present not to have despaired of Dada, and it is rather touching to think that he is liable to remain Dada's plaything until the day he dies, as we saw Jarry remain the plaything of Ubu. This is another of his charming

---

5. A reference to Boulanger (1837–91), charismatic leader of a radical political party, who lost face when he hesitated to lead a coup d'état against the French government. In 1889 he fled to Belgium to avoid arrest and two years later killed himself in disgrace on the tomb of his mistress. (trans.)

confusions, which can pass—in this domain where the greatest clairvoyance does no more than push back the darkness a bit—for the finest thing of all. I do believe that examples of such confusions, from which Philippe Soupault's works take much of their flavor, can readily be found in his life as well.

On the other hand, Louis Aragon and Paul Eluard—the former making light of the difficulties, the latter with infinite prudence—are already heading toward something else. Aragon, who more easily than anyone escapes minor daily disaster, and Eluard, who by dint of taking his inspiration from it makes us see it as his own revenge, have control over the future and charge into the fray from both sides at the same time. On the one hand, Aragon's stories, his terrible anecdotes, those little films where everything turns out so badly, were placed before our eyes just in time; on the other, Eluard's poems, which are punctuated by nights of love and act as the sheath over our secret, are another reason to live—that is, they both encourage and exasperate our patience.

Benjamin Péret, as long as he constructs his own stories and poems, in which the burlesque of modern life truly explodes for the first time in a spirit devoid of bitterness as in the comedies of Mack Sennett (the most mysterious thing the movies have yet offered us), is not living up to his full potential. I have no hesitation in saying that he is one of the people I am most moved to know. I sometimes go so far as to envy him his remarkable lack of "structure" and his perpetual drifting.

With Jacques Baron, who is seventeen, it is impossible not to look even more toward the future. Moreover, this is all we have tried to do here. And too strange a seduction emanates from Jacques Baron's poetry for me to resist it this time, that poetry in which

> *Corpses who were funny*
> *Get drunk and charm lovers*
> *Lovers who have flowers*
> *Covered with ink or dust*

Gentlemen, in this plain I no longer see anyone but Robert Desnos, the knight who has so far ridden furthest of all. . . . To me it seems certain that before long the new lyricism that I have tried to characterize this evening, and that involves—as you must have noticed—something entirely different from the so-called new conditions that machinism, for instance, has imposed on life; it seems certain, I say, that this new lyricism will find ways of expressing itself without the help of books—which does not mean, as Apollinaire foolishly thought, that it will replace them with the phonograph. For that, there is only one man freed from all constraints, like Robert Desnos, who will be able to carry the torch far enough. I will make just one wish in closing, which is that my enormous affection for him will not prove so heavy that he cannot keep performing miracles with his eyes closed.

And this, gentlemen, is what is happening in Paris, very late, after the art and other galleries close for the night. All the rest— in other words, everything that is being said about a classical renaissance (explain yourselves!), about a return to nature (spare me the idiocy), and about the serious labor that consists in copying fruits because, alas! that's what sells, or in adding one more petty little state of mind, which is the only way to pass for a right-thinking individual—is absolutely null and void. And you must also realize that I had no wish to leave even the narrowest margin next to what I've just said. Paraphrasing a famous statement, I am tempted to add that there is no purgatory for the mind.[6] And on these words, gentlemen, permit me to take my leave.

6. Breton is paraphrasing the "revelation" of Abbé Tussert (in Villiers de l'Isle-Adam's story "L'Enjeu"). According to Tussert, the Church's best-kept secret is that "there is no Purgatory." (trans.)

Sources and Acknowledgments

In the interests of style and accuracy, I have occasionally revised (without further indication) some of the previously published translations cited herein.

The Disdainful Confession
First published as "La Confession dédaigneuse" in the political monthly *La Vie moderne* (in several installments, February–March 1923). Much of this essay was adapted from letters that Breton had written to his employer of the time, the dress designer and arts patron Jacques Doucet, for whom he worked as curator and cultural interpreter from 1920 to 1924.

Excerpts from the letters of Jacques Vaché are based on translations by Martin Sorrell.

Guillaume Apollinaire
First published in *L'Eventail* (15 October 1918).

Extracts of poems from *Alcools* and *Calligrammes* are translated by Anne Hyde Greet, in Guillaume Apollinaire, *Alcools* (Berkeley: University of California Press, 1965) and *Calligrammes: Poems of Peace and War (1913–1916)* (Berkeley: University of California Press, 1980). Lines from "The Musician of Saint-Merry" and "The Song of the Poorly-Loved" are translated by Roger Shattuck, in *The Selected Writings of Guillaume Apollinaire* (New York: New Directions, 1958). Excerpts from *The Poet Assassinated* are translated by Ron Padgett, in *The Poet Assassinated and Other Stories* (Berkeley: North Point, 1984). Excerpt from "Que Vlove?" is translated by Rémy Inglis Hall, in *The Heresiarch and Co.* (Cambridge, MA: Exact Change, 1991). Lines from "The Pont Mirabeau" are translated by Richard Wilbur, in Paul Auster, ed.,

The Random House Book of Twentieth-Century French Poetry (New York: Random House, 1982). Poems from *Bestiary* are translated by Pepe Karmel, in *Bestiary or The Parade of Orpheus* (Boston: David R. Godine, 1980). I also acknowledge translations by Lionel Abel (*The Cubist Painters*) and Wallace Fowlie (Rimbaud).

Alfred Jarry
First published in *Les Ecrits nouveaux* (January 1919).
   "The pubic arch of menhirs" and excerpts from *Exploits and Opinions of Doctor Faustroll, Pataphysician* are translated by Simon Watson Taylor. "The Royal Toilet" is translated by Stanley Chapman. Excerpt from *Les Polyèdres* and the song of the Palcontents are adapted from similar scenes in *Ubu Cuckolded,* translated by Cyril Connolly. All selections are contained in *Selected Works of Alfred Jarry,* ed. Roger Shattuck and Simon Watson Taylor (New York: Grove, 1965).

Jacques Vaché
First published as the preface to Vaché's *Lettres de guerre* (Paris: Au Sans Pareil, 1919).

Two Dada Manifestoes
First published in *Littérature* 13 (May 1920) under the individual titles "Dada Geography" and "Dada Ice-Skating."

The Cantos of Maldoror
First published as "Les Chants de Maldoror" in *La Nouvelle Revue Française* (1 June 1920).
   Excerpts from *Maldoror* are translated by Alexis Lykiard, in *Maldoror and the Complete Works of the Comte de Lautréamont* (Cambridge, MA: Exact Change, 1994).

For Dada
First published as "Pour Dada" in *La Nouvelle Revue Française* (1 August 1920).

   Excerpts from "Dada Manifesto 1918" are translated by Barbara Wright, in Tristan Tzara, *Seven Dada Manifestos and Lampisteries* (London: John Calder, 1977).

Gaspard de la Nuit
First published in *La Nouvelle Revue Française* (1 September 1920).

Max Ernst
First published in the catalog to an exhibit of Ernst's drawings and collages (Paris, Au Sans Pareil bookstore, 3 May–3 June 1921).

Ideas of a Painter
First published as "Idées d'un peintre" in *Littérature* 18 (March 1921).

Giorgio de Chirico
First published in *Littérature* 11 (January 1920).

André Gide Speaks to Us of His Selected Works
First published as "André Gide nous parle de ses morceaux choisis" in *Littérature*, new ser., 1 (1 March 1922).

Interview with Doctor Freud
First published as "Interview du Professeur Freud" in *Littérature*, new ser., 1 (1 March 1922).

The New Spirit
First published as "L'Esprit nouveau" in *Littérature*, new ser., 1 (1 March 1922).

After Dada
First published as "Après dada" in *Comoedia* (2 March 1922).

Leave Everything
First published as "Lâchez tout" in *Littérature*, new ser., 2 (1 April 1922).

Clearly
First published as "Clairement" in *Littérature*, new ser., 4 (1 September 1922).

Reply to a Survey
First published as "Réponse à une enquête" in *Le Figaro* (21 May 1922).

Marcel Duchamp
First published in *Littérature,* new ser., 5 (1 October 1922).

The Mediums Enter
First published as "Entrée des médiums" in *Littérature,* new ser., 6 (1 November 1922). The magazine version contained more extensive transcripts of the séances.

Francis Picabia
First published in the catalog to an exhibit of Picabia's works (Barcelona, Dalmau gallery, 18 November–8 December 1922).

Words without Wrinkles
First published as "Les Mots sans rides" in *Littérature,* new ser., 7 (1 December 1922).

Distance
First published as "Distances" in *Paris-Journal* (23 March 1923).

Characteristics of the Modern Evolution
Previously unpublished. Originally delivered as a lecture on the evening before Picabia's exhibit of watercolors opened at the Dalmau gallery, Barcelona.

Excerpts from Lautréamont's *Maldoror* are translated by Alexis Lykiard. Lines from Rimbaud's "What Does It Matter?" are translated by Wallace Fowlie, in Arthur Rimbaud, *Complete Works, Selected Letters* (Chicago: University of Chicago Press, 1966). Lines from Apollinaire's "Monday on Rue Christine" are translated by Anne Hyde Greet, in *Calligrammes.* Excerpt from Tzara's "Open Letter to Jacques Rivière" is translated by Barbara Wright, in *Seven Dada Manifestos.*

Index of Names

www.ingramcontent.com/pod-product-compliance
Ingram Content Group UK Ltd.
Pitfield, Milton Keynes, MK11 3LW, UK
UKHW032342180125
453882UK00001B/2